THE BEE KEEPERS

THE BEE KEEPERS

JAN CHEAL

authorHOUSE®

AuthorHouse™
1663 Liberty Drive
Bloomington, IN 47403
www.authorhouse.com
Phone: 1-800-839-8640

This is a work of fiction. All of the characters, names, incidents, organizations, and dialogue in this novel are either the products of the author's imagination or are used fictitiously.

Published by AuthorHouse   03/15/2013

ISBN: 978-1-4817-8777-2 (sc)
ISBN: 978-1-4817-8778-9 (e)

In loving memory of my dear friend Grace Shaw

CHAPTER ONE

They had both fallen in love at first sight with Carrow Mansions, a fine two storey Victorian property which displayed all the usual traits for a house of that period with a bay window, iron railings and Flemish brick bonding that was complete with coloured patterned brickwork. The front doorway and windows had stained glass and a grey slate tiled roof that completed No. 27 Hereford Row in the city of Durham.

A leaflet for the property had fallen through their door from the property agent Ross and Bailey in the New Year and a subsequent visit had confirmed their anticipation and in their own words ticked every box. A few months later Richard Fellowes, his wife Susan and 15 year old daughter Robyn moved in lock stock and barrel. They loved their house in Notting Hill where they had lived for the past 10 years but the arm of the British Beekeepers Association dealing solely with viruses, and to whom Richard was affiliated, had relocated to Durham as part of a cost cutting exercise. Like many other companies and organisations they had felt the impact of the downturn in the financial market that meant every penny counted and the rental costs of office accommodation in the big city were stretching that resource just a bit too far. The British Beekeepers Association had acquired some modest premises in the city centre where Brian Dawes his boss, George Myers who worked closely with Richard and Piers Marchmont an Associate Director were now housed.

Richard usually put in a four hour day at the office but another attraction that Carrow Mansions held for him was the small laboratory he had managed to create at the back of the house. The deeds to the property revealed that when it was first built in 1860, the heyday of religion in Victorian Britain, it was occupied by a Reverend Bates who used the house as a presbytery. At the back a small room had been made into a chapel complete with stained glass windows where no doubt the Reverend pondered and sweated over his Sunday sermons. In subsequent years it had been used as a storage area by different occupants and now with a few benches, cupboards and experimental flasks and bottles had become Richard's laboratory where he could pursue his never ending study of bee viruses. At first his boss Brian had expressed doubts about his working from home, always a stickler for protocol and convention, but eventually had been won over after a visit to Carrow Mansions and a mini tour of the small laboratory. Ironically despite his initial doubts he saw the benefit of this arrangement and knowing how devoted Richard was to his work envisaged that the advantages would far outweigh the disadvantages to the BBKA.

It was on a Thursday, the 4th March to be precise, after Richard received a telephone call from the Veterinary Medicines Directorate who they worked closely with, that the wheels were set in motion for a series of incidents that were wholly inexplicable. It had been a very busy day and a request late in the afternoon had led to Richard agreeing to carry out an experiment at home that evening. The ailments and illnesses of bees was multi disciplined and ranged from pests and parasites, bacterial diseases, fungal diseases and viral diseases. The latter was the one to which Richard now applied himself and in particular the acute bee paralysis virus that incorporated the Kashmir Bee Virus also known as KBV. Little was known about it and the only way of positively identifying it was by laboratory tests. There would not usually have been the urgency for this information but a seminar was being held the following week and the papers were in the throes of preparation and an update was needed as soon as possible.

Richard replaced the telephone in its cradle and rubbed his forehead. 'There isn't much time to sort this one out so I think I'll make tracks and get started as soon as I can'.

Brian walked out of his office as Richard gathered some papers together and stuffed them in his brief case. 'Yes please, I always like to keep the VMD happy and it gives us some brownie points' he added. He smiled to himself and thought yes, despite my initial doubts this home laboratory has turned out to be a godsend. 'Give me a call later Richard, time permitting, to let me know how it goes'.

Richard waived his arm in a positive response as he disappeared around the doorway to make his way to the lift that quickly whisked him to the ground floor below. The walk to the car park was a short one and on his way he slipped into a local off licence to pick up a bottle of valpolicella, a favourite tipple of his, and smiled to himself thinking that he would treat himself to a few glasses later than evening after he had finished his homework naturally.

CHAPTER TWO

The first part of Richard's journey was slow due to an articulated lorry that had decided to break down right in the middle of the main thoroughfare out of the city centre, and a young policeman with a harried expression on his face was doing his best to hurry the impatient traffic past the stationary vehicle. Once he got past the hold up Richard put his foot down and quickly sped into the suburbs of Durham and through its leafy lanes, for not only did he love his new home but also the drive to and from work and decided that it was a vast improvement to the hustle and bustle of the London underground.

As he pulled up at the front of 27 Hereford Row he spotted the tail end of Susan's car pulling off with Robyn waving out of the back window. He remembered that it was Thursday and her night for dancing classes at the local academy. It was Robyn's dream to be a professional dancer and have her name in lights and they both always did what they could to support her. Richard reached for his brief case out of the back seat of the car not forgetting to retrieve his bottle of wine neatly wrapped in a single layer of thin tissue paper.

Susan had left a note for him on the kitchen table saying that she had left a rather nice beef casserole in the oven that would be ready whenever he was. Perfect he thought to himself, that would give him a good few hours to complete his task. He was feeling a bit jaded and decided that a good strong cup of coffee would perk him up in readiness for his work next door as he flicked the switch on the side of the kettle. While he waited for it to boil he went over in his mind what he needed to do and hoped that he had remembered all the relevant paperwork. A few moments later armed with his shot of caffeine, Richard made his way through the kitchen door and into the passageway at the back that led into the laboratory, a small room measuring some 12 feet by 10 feet but compact. One of the things he had first noticed when they viewed the property was how this room had retained its fine Victorian wall tiles, the green and maroon colours so vibrant, in fact the majority of the house had been left untouched and escaped the clutches of the DIY brigade that were so prevalent these days.

Richard took a sip of his coffee and reached over to open his brief case where he retrieved a large bundle of papers comprising of graphs and various write-ups by other bee specialists on the Kashmir Bee Virus and their opinions as to this terrible paralysis and possible ultimate demise of the species. It had become so serious that this special seminar had been called at short notice to discuss preventative measures on how to stop it spreading. The average person thought Richard had no idea that aside from the loss of a jar of honey at their dining table, several crops key to human life would be wiped out like the soya bean, cotton, brassicas, brazil nuts and almonds, grapes, apples and sunflowers, the source of a large amount of the world's vegetable oil. Almost a third of the world's food was traceable to the action of bees and it was envisaged that if they became extinct severe food shortages would follow with starvation and violence on a massive scale.

On a large shelf at the back of his desk were two large microscopes one of which he now placed firmly in front of him ready for the glass slide to be inserted under the lens. The last task now was to place a poor victim of KBV on the slide after of course some necessary dissection. He swung round in his chair and reached onto a shelf behind him where a wooden box sat serving as a temporary mortuary for his apis mellifera. With the finest pair of tweezers he extracted a bee and carefully placed it onto the lens and made it ready for the next stage that involved the separation of the body from the wings. He always marvelled at the beauty of their wings, so tiny and exquisite like tracing paper but with perfect symmetrical venation. He squinted his eyes and noticed that the light was fading fast now and leaned over to turn on another examination light at the back of the bench. He saw that the weather outside had become very blustery as he noticed the branch of a tree swinging wildly as it was reflected by the moon on the wall in front of him from the window behind. Suddenly he was aware of a sharp piercing sensation in his lower arm and looking down saw that the bee which had been on the microscope lens was now clinging on to him and inflicting the nastiest of stings. Richard brushed the bee onto the desk and briskly rubbed the painful spot near his wrist which had already started to throb. He remembered that he had spotted half a large onion on the kitchen table, a remnant from the meal that Susan had prepared earlier that afternoon, and that the acid would provide a natural antidote to his current predicament. As he looked up and his eyes met the wall in front of him he noticed that the strangest of things had happened. The branch that had been wildly waving around had now gone and the clearest, palest moon ever shone onto the wall, what the hell was going on. He walked over towards the door but found that it was no longer there and everything was different. The bright piercing examination lights had disappeared and been replaced by a deep red glow from a massive fireplace that was burning some twenty feet away illuminating a large hall. He looked up and saw above him a tall rib-vaulted ceiling that was supported by two enormous columns, and his nostrils detected a pervading musty smell accompanied by the aroma of wood ash from a huge fire that was burning in the hearth. Sheer blind terror overcame him now and he started to panic, aware that his heart was pounding in his chest. He took some deep breaths to steady himself and then noticed two figures who were sitting in front of the fireplace who were engrossed in deep conversation and as he walked over towards them one of the figures stood up and looked straight at him.

He tried to speak but nothing came out, his mouth was bone dry and swallowing deeply suddenly found his voice. 'Where, where the hell am I and who are you' he stammered. He quickly realised though that he had not been seen or heard as the figure now turned back towards the fire and continued his conversation with the other man. He must be invisible, they could not see him. What was going on? Richard moved nearer to them and now saw at close hand that the man who had stared at him was wearing a monk's habit with a cowl and his head was shaven with a ring of hair around the crown. The other man, still sat by the fire and wore a short peasant like tunic with a shawl around his shoulders and unlike his companion his hair was longer and he had a short beard.

'One thing is for sure Conan things cannot carry on as they are. Our abbot Linus Deyer is bleeding our coffers dry by the day'.

'Yes you are right Adolphus' he replied. 'And this latest piece of news about heavy borrowing from this Jewish money lenders will make things even worse as they are renowned for such fraud. I think he has lost his senses and too old for the task, they say that with age comes wisdom but not here maybe.' This question was left hanging in the air.

Richard now stared straight into their faces where the reflection of the fire flickered on their tough leather like skin. Adolphus appeared to be the elder of the two, around middle age Richard guessed while the other man was younger. A sudden noise at the other end of the hall caught Richard's attention as he turned to see two other figures who had walked in through a large wooden door. He walked silently as a ghost towards them and started to witness some medical process that looked positively medieval. On a table a large bowl had been placed over which another monk had placed his arm and an incision made by his companion. Blood slowly dripped into the receptacle and after a few moments a cloth was wrapped around the wound tightly. Richard wiped his brow for what he had witnessed was bleeding, the ancient form of blood letting to maintain and improve good health.

He peered out of the door that he now stood next to and saw what looked like a large cloister over the other side of which he gazed onto the huge mullioned windows of a large cathedral. He decided to explore further but he suddenly felt someone grip his shoulders from behind and thought to himself that despite his earlier misgivings he had been seen. As he turned round he looked up expecting to see the leather like face of one of the monks but instead was staring straight into Susan's eyes that were wide open with surprise and alarm.

'Richard what's happened, are you alright' she said.

Richard shook his head and looked around him, the blazing fire and tall rib-vaulted ceiling had disappeared and he was now back in his small laboratory at Carrow Mansions. Susan though very worried was looking at him like a naughty schoolboy.

'When I walked in the room you were just standing there looking into space, I wondered if you had had some kind of seizure' she said. 'I spoke to you but you couldn't hear me, or see me either' she added.

Although Susan didn't know it he thought to himself she was absolutely right, because what she didn't know and couldn't know is that he wasn't there at all, he was back somewhere in a previous time where he moved as a ghost amongst others. One thing though was certain and that was he did not want to talk about what had happened to him. He needed time to think and try and make some kind of sense of it all.

'I was just starting to carry out my experiment when I was stung by a dam bee. I was sure it was dead but it must have been comatose'. He raised his wrist for her to see the painful swollen spot that still smarted'.

'I'll get something for that' she told him and went onto inform him that if he didn't eat properly this kind of thing was going to happen. 'Just a snatched sandwich for lunch and half the meals I cook for you in the evening are only picked at'. She fell silent then and decided that the lecture was over for now but would definitely be continued another time. After administering some lotion to his arm he was promptly marched up stairs, assisted into his striped pyjamas and put to bed.

'We'll see how you are tomorrow and I might call in the doctor if I'm still not happy' she said.

'Don't fuss so much, I'll be fine' Richard replied. 'I just need a good night's sleep and I will be right as rain tomorrow' he concluded. Susan extinguished the bedside light and went back downstairs. He lay there in the dark thinking to himself that he would need more than a few good meals to sort this thing out but now he must rest, he felt exhausted and had a bad headache that was starting to throb rather badly.

CHAPTER THREE

He awoke the next morning still with a headache that had become rather dull now as Susan came into the bedroom with a large tray. She pulled back the curtains and looked at him for a few minutes. 'I don't want any arguments now, you're to eat all of this' she told him. She placed in front of him a plate laden with eggs, bacon and tomatoes accompanied by two large rounds of toast. He found in fact that he was rather hungry and much to her satisfaction polished it all off while she sat on the edge of the bed next to him. 'How are you feeling' she asked and was informed that he was fine, just over tired. She looked suspiciously at him but decided to leave their chat to another time much to Richard's relief.

As he showered in the privacy of the bathroom Richard pondered the events of the previous evening. Everything had been fine until he was stung by the bee, it was something to do with that, but what. One minute he was in his laboratory and the next somewhere completely different, somewhere back in time. He needed to do some urgent research, not about bees this time but rather an historical one. Who was Linus Deyer, the abbot and also Adolphus and Conan come

11

to that. Had he somehow dreamed the whole thing or were they actual people who had existed. He then remembered that because of his, what would he call it, journey perhaps for now, the research work urgently required had been left completely untouched. He wiped his brow and decided that he would simply tell them that due to a nasty gastric attack he had been confined to the bathroom all evening, yes that would do it plus of course the bee sting.

Susan was waiting at the bottom of the stairs with a large package in her hands. 'What's that' said Richard as he reached for his coat off the peg in the hallway.

'It's your lunch and also your favourite, tuna salad sandwiches and you must eat them, I shall ask you tonight and I always know if your not telling me the truth' she said. Richard cast his eyes down and hoped that wasn't really the case as he had a feeling he was going to be telling quite a few stories from now on one way or another.

'Yes and dutifully promise I shall eat it all' he said. 'I must just fetch my papers from the laboratory' he said as he made his way through the hall to his small room at the back of the house. He closed the door behind him and looked around the room and especially through the window behind him. The tree was there now, still waiving around in a strong breeze, but where was it last night Richard thought to himself. This thing, whatever it was, seemed to be taking over and pulling himself together grabbed the sheath of papers from his desk that were totally unread from last night. After one more look he quietly closed the door behind him and made his way to the front door. 'I'll be off then, see you tonight' he called over his shoulder as he left the house and climbed into his car on the driveway.

The first part of his journey through the suburbs was fine but as he approached the main thoroughfare into the city centre he saw that there was yet another hold up. Last night it had been a lorry but today there had been a rather nasty collision between two cars that also involved a motorcyclist. It was some way up in front and judging by the speed the traffic was moving guessed he would be in for rather a long wait. He turned his engine off and his mind soon started to wander, back to last night. Had he been some kind of time traveller via a chemical reaction from the bee sting, was it all an hallucination or perhaps it was just some kind of breakdown. It had all seemed so real and wondered if his return to the present day was after he had been touched by Susan? If she hadn't found him then would he still be there, wherever there was? He wasn't too sure how he felt about the prospect but at the same time was hugely excited, dare he say it, about going back again, that was indeed if he ever could. A loud blast sounded in his ears from the car behind him and looking in the rear view mirror saw an irate motorist behind him rudely gesticulating. He quickly turned on the ignition and put the car into first gear to begin the snail's pace past the accident further up the road.

An hour or so later Richard deposited his vehicle in the nearby car park and some few minutes later walked into the reception of his office building where Ted who manned the front desk called out to him 'Early today Mr Fellowes, couldn't sleep'. Richard waived his arm in some kind of response to him as he entered the ground floor lift that would take him up to the 5th floor. George Myers a colleague of Richard spotted him as he walked into the office and made a point of coming over to have a chat with him. George was mid 40's and married to Lisa with two daughters and although a nice enough chap Richard always considered him rather dull. He blamed his wife Lisa, such a dominating woman and quite vein too sometimes he thought. He would never end up like that, Susan liked to dominate him sometimes but there were limits and they both knew it, an invisible line that was never crossed.

'You look tired Richard' George said 'Have you been up burning the midnight oil working on this research paper'. Richard looked up at George and really wished that that had been the case'.

'No as a matter of fact I had a nasty gastric stomach and was stung by a bee'.

'Oh' George replied looking at him in a quizzical way'.

'Yes so I have a lot of catching up to do' Richard replied as he slipped into his seat and pulled some papers out of his brief case.

'Well I'll leave you to it' George said, 'can I get you some coffee'.

'No your alright, just going to get sorted out here and then see the old man' Richard said. The old man he referred to was Brian Dawes, his boss. Richard quite liked Brian and had always got on well with him, not just professionally but on a personal level too. He had always enjoyed his company when they were away on trips and forced to spend time together in the evenings that invariably ended up in a local bar.

Richard hesitated slightly before knocking on Brian's door and waited for the usual response of enter. Brian looked up and immediately informed Richard that he didn't look well.

'Yes I wasn't good last night, gastric trouble plus a bee sting' he said.

'Oh' Brian said, 'bad luck'.

'The point is that because of my incapacities I didn't have a chance to do this research work last night'. He fell silent and looked down. 'However' he continued, 'I shall more than make up for it today, hence my early arrival'.

'Yes I wondered what you were doing here so dammed early, well I won't waste any more of your time, off with you and make sure you do a good job'.

'Yes skipper' Richard replied and slipped out of the lion's den back to his desk. George was hanging about obviously waiting for some feedback after his meeting with the boss. 'Loads to do George, no time to chat now' Richard said quickly getting rid of him as he sat down. George took the hint and wandered over and busied himself with making a cup of coffee for himself. Richard shut his eyes for a few moments and tried to focus, he was finding it difficult to concentrate and scooping everything up into his arms decided to retreat to the sanctuary of laboratory No. 1. 'If there are any calls for me just take a message' he shouted as he made his escape out of the main office and down the corridor.

He breathed a sigh of relief as he closed the laboratory door behind him and started to repeat the same process as last night, that was before he had been interrupted by the bee sting that had consequently led to his trip. First he would read the research data and then complete the dissection. The data was endless with opinions and theories from numerous specialists on the acute bee paralysis virus. A common theory for the virus was attributed to pollen and nectar from plants such as buttercups, rhododendrons, laurel and some species of basswood. Also a deficiency in pollen during breeding in the early spring and the consumption of stored fermented pollen appeared to be culprits. The consensus seemed to be that the means of spreading the virus was by secretions from the bees' salivary glands. He pulled out a chart and noted the virus code for

ABPV 00.101.0.00.006 and the genome sequence accession number AY150629. He tapped his pen on the edge of the desk and prepared himself for the final part of the exercise. Over in the corner of the room a small fridge stood on a shelf where the deceased apis mellifera were kept. Richard opened the fridge door and carefully retrieved a plastic box containing two dead bees. One of them was now placed under the microscope and Richard prodded the bee with a pair of tweezers, he wasn't taking any chances this time. The bee lay inert on the slide and he noted it was bald as one of the side effects was loss of hair from their bodies as well as a dark, shiny and greasy appearance. He wondered if the chemical reaction that had caused his trip only came from bees with this virus and knew the only way he would find out was by another sting. This idea quickened his heart beat and he quickly stopped his train of thought and addressed the paper he now had to write, there would be plenty of time for that later.

Some two hours later he emerged triumphantly from the laboratory somewhat relieved it was all over. As his boss read the last page of his work he looked up at Richard beaming, 'Good work, good work, I know I can always rely on you Richard and it is such an important issue, in simple terms what may happen to the world's food supply. The wars in the future won't be about territory, no mark my word they will be about food and water too' he added.

'Yes well apart from the obvious technical element I wanted to make the point but keep it fairly low key in some areas' Richard said.

'I can see that and you have achieved it admirably' said Brian. 'Do you fancy a quick drink before you go, I'm assuming your soon be off after your early start etc.'

'Thanks Brian but no thanks, I have a few things to do so I'll just say goodbye and see you on Monday, have a good weekend'.

'You too, and don't' get stung by any more bees' Brian said as Richard walked out of the door. Richard couldn't help smiling to himself because although Brian didn't know it, that was exactly what he intended to do, and sooner rather than later.

CHAPTER FOUR

Back at Carrow Mansions Richard went through the routine of checking the post and the ansaphone for any messages, almost in some way delaying the moment he could hardly wait for. The house was silent as Friday was Susan's day at a local charity shop for the aged, she often told Richard rather depressingly that maybe one day they would be in need of their help and so she was doing her bit now. Nothing could be heard apart from the loud tick of the grandfather clock that stood in the hall and the pendulum that swung back and forth. He knew that this was the point of no return, either he would find nothing in which case that would be an end to it or, he would find something and if so his course was set.

He switched his computer on and waited patiently for the home page to appear. He clicked on the google site and held his breath as his fingers typed abbot Linus Deyer and pushed the enter key. A few moments later he watched as page after page flashed up on the screen the result of which he knew would decide his fate. He fidgeted restless for the computer to finish downloading and remembered the bottle of valpolicella from the other night that he had totally forgotten about after everything that had happened. He went into the kitchen and fetched a large wine glass from one of the cupboards and poured a good measure of the deep red liquid for himself. In one mouthful it was gone and he refilled the glass again before returning to the sitting room. As he walked in the door he saw the computer screen was now still and google had completed its task.

Richard scrolled the pages down with a lot of factual information and realised that what he saw before him now was none other than an account, an historical account of the Cistercian order at Fountains Abbey in Ripon. His eyes flicked over the data concerning the historical background and a description of the plans and buildings until he reached a section listing the Abbots from its inception in 1132 to its dissolution in 1539 when Henry VIII closed all the monasteries. He already knew that Linus Deyer's name was included on the list of those abbots on the next screen, over the page whatever you cared to call it thanks to the wonders of modern technology and the search engine google. He decided to be patient and would methodically work his way down the list until he found what he was looking for, however tempting it was to do otherwise.

1132-1139 Richard I, former prior of St Mary at York. Elected as the first abbot of Fountains, so called as the humble origins of the abbey were in the narrow valley of the little River Skell where springs of good water flowed from the rocks.

1139-1143 Richard II, sacrist of York, prior of Fountains., an unworldly and retiring man who shrank from the administrative duties imposed on him by his office and suffered from a nervous stammer. It was the misfortune of this shy man to embroil Fountains in a damaging public controversy over the succession to the see of York. Archbishop Thurstan died in 1140 and King Stephen procured the election of William Fitzherbert to the archbishopric. The Augustinians and Cistercians were strongly opposed to this outcome and with the aid of St Bernard and on the strength of evidence given by Abbot Richard II in Rome, they managed to persuade the pope to withhold recognition of the election. In the midst of this controversy Abbot Richard II died when visiting Clairvaux.

1144-1147 Henry Murdac abbot of Vauclair, was sent to England to advise the convent in the election of a new abbot but was actually elected himself. He was a zealot and forceful character and the first abbot of Fountains to have been trained in continental Cisterican practices and set about reforming the abbey and ridding it of the last remnants of Benedictine customs. Under his rule the convent flourished and grew in numbers and was responsible for much building work including the aisled nave.

1147-1148 Maurice subprior of Durham, abbot of Rievaulx, a scholar of repute who was Abbot for only three months.

1148-1150 Thorold monk of Rievaulx and subsequently abbot of Trois-Fountaines, considered too independent for the domineering archbishop's liking and was removed from office by St Bernard.

1150-1170 Richard III, precentor of Clairvaux, abbot of Vauclair, a native of York who led an austere life. In his early years he faced dissension amongst his monks and expelled the ringleaders of the opposition. He ruled for twenty years and by the time of his death Fountains along with Byland and Rievaulx were known as the three shining lights of the Order in England.

1170-1180 Robert of Pipewell, abbot of Pipewell, a capable administrator who ruled firmly and well, leaving behind a name for hospitality to rich and poor alike.

Richard now drew a very deep breath as he eyes moved to the next entry.

1180-1185 Linus Deyer, monk of Rievaulx, a man whose ambitions were outweighed by his shortcomings. He held the previous abbot Henry Murdac in very high esteem and used him as a role model. Due to mismanagement of funds he managed to plunge the abbey into a financial mire and was removed from office.

1185-1187 Henry Cuylter, sacrist of York, a very practical man who managed to turn the fortunes round for Fountains. Due to poor health his tenure as abbot was unfortunately a short one.

Richard had been holding his breath as he read the last two entries and now gave a long gasp. There it was without a shadow of a doubt, Linus Deyer did exist, had existed, he became temporarily confused as it seemed the past and the present so easily rolled into one. He had listened to that conversation between Adolphus and Conan by the fireplace as they discussed the shortcomings of Linus and his mismanagement of the abbey. What he knew and they didn't know was Linus was deposed in 1185, he took office in 1180 for five years, but what year was he there? He knew that he just had to find out and went through the plan he had put in place at work that morning, the how, where and when. Before he left the laboratory earlier that day he had taken two of the ailing bees, quite comatose and deposited them in a container in his briefcase ready for the sting. The where would be the same place as before in the small room at the back of the house, and the when would be tomorrow as Susan by a stroke of good fortune was spending the weekend with her sister Frances and her family in Whitley Bay, he would have the house to himself. It couldn't have worked out better, even Robyn wasn't going to be there as she was staying with one of her friends.

He pulled the screen down on his computer and heard the click as it shut tightly. The loud hollow chime of the grandfather clock in the halllway told him it was 6 o'clock and Susan would soon be home with a takeaway, she never cooked on a Friday and chicken dansak with pillau rice had become a weekly ritual for them. He pulled a checked table cloth out of the sideboard and smoothed it carefully over the table. There was no guarantee of course that it would work, he could recreate the circumstances but that was all and the rest was down to fate. As he laid the last piece of cutlery on the table he heard the front door open and Susan call out that she was home and hoped the table was ready.

'Yes it's all done' said Richard as she walked in the room and eyed the set table first and then Richard.

'So I see, anyone would think you were trying to impress me, you're not up to anything are you, a guilty conscience' she said looking at him out of the corner of her eyes.

'No darling of course not, I just wanted to help out'. She wasn't far from the truth actually as he remembered their conversation yesterday when she told him that she had a feeling something was going on but she didn't know what. Poor Susan, if she only knew what had happened and moreover what was going to happen she would be absolutely horrified.

Richard opened the containers and started to spoon the curry onto the plates as he heard Susan say 'I'll be leaving about midday tomorrow and should be home at 5 o'clock on Sunday. Now come on lets eat before it gets cold'.

CHAPTER FIVE

It was the rays of bright sunlight filtering through the curtains in the bedroom window that woke Richard, he quietly turned and saw that the digital bedside clock said it was 8.30 am. He looked over his shoulder and saw that Susan was still safely in the arms of Morpheus as the bedclothes gently rose and fell. He laid back down and looked at the rose and lavender wallpaper that was really quite hideous, another job on his list of to-do's but it would have to wait. At the moment he hadn't got the time, yes time that elusive thing, you can't see it, you can't touch it, your just aware of it as he had been yesterday in his transportation back to 800 years ago. He thought of other time travellers like HG Wells whose method of transportation was a machine and Dr Who a telephone box, for him it had been a bee sting. Any further thought was disturbed as he heard a quiet knock on the bedroom door and Robyn walked in with a tray of morning tea for them.

'Morning dad, thought you and mum would appreciate a cuppa' she said.

'Yes thanks love, what time are you off to Eve's today' Richard enquired.

'Soon actually, we're going into town to do some serious shopping, mostly window though unfortunately. Just wait till I make it to the big time, it will Rodeo Drive for me in the USA.' she said.

Richard laughed 'Be off with you, and remember behave.'

'Ok dad' Robyn replied in a resolute way and waved her hand behind her as she walked out the door.

Susan moaned and gave a huge stretch struggling to open her eyes. They had been married for twenty years and he wondered where that time had gone. They had met at university and been attracted to each other at first sight and unlike some relationships that blossomed and fizzled out theirs didn't and they duly married. Some two years later Robyn was born and everything was complete.

'Ah you're with us, cup of tea Susan' he said.

She didn't speak but simply nodded yes and gradually sat up in bed. She loved the weekends and wherever possible did everything as slow as possible to make things last. After a few moments and a few sips of tea she gave Richard some jobs that she wanted him to do while the house was empty, including a trip to the local library as there were four books already overdue. After promising that she needn't worry as he would take care of everything, Richard went into the bathroom for a quick shower and to work out his timetable for the day. Susan was leaving at midday so as soon as she left he would go to the library and then come back home finish the other chores and hopefully be finished by 4 o'clock. Then it would be time, time for his sting. He wondered if it would work again and also, more importantly, if he would be transported back to the same time as before.

He could hardly wait for Susan to go and sat through an agonisingly long breakfast making small talk over the bacon and scrambled eggs. After the second cafetiere of coffee Richard pointed at his wristwatch reminding Susan that she should be making tracks as the Saturday shoppers had a terrible habit of clogging up all the roads.

'Don't fuss so Richard, it's a straight forward run out the city centre onto the A690 which runs into the A19 and turn right at the top. Anyone would think you were trying to get rid of me, have you got a secret rendezvous here with a loose woman' she said. It was true he did have a rendezvous though not with a woman but the monks at Fountains Abbey in the 12th century.

'No don't be silly it's just that I don't want you to have to rush, the roads are just a nightmare these days' he said.

'I take the hint' she said and drained her coffee cup. 'Just going to pack a few things and I'll be out of your hair'. When she had gone upstairs Richard swiftly cleared the table and loaded the dishwasher. He pressed a button and listened to the gentle whirl of the water as it filled the drum and then the slow hum of the motor. If something happened again today he was considering letting Brian into the secret, who knows perhaps they could take a trip together and compare notes afterwards.

He felt an arm around his neck as Susan planted a long kiss on his cheek. 'I'll ring you tonight to let you know I'm ok'.

'Yes take care love, drive carefully and I'll see you tomorrow afternoon' Richard said. He stood at the front door until her car turned the corner of the road and disappeared out of sight. The house was now quiet and it reminded Richard of the theatre, when the lights went down low and a silent hush fell over the audience. The stage was set.

Richard walked at a fast pace down Hereford Row and into Graham Road, it was a delightful walk and much to look at but not today. It was his first visit to their local library that was located on a medium sized square near the outskirts of the town. He admired the fine red brickwork of the Victorian building with its huge windows as he walked up the front steps and a cursory glance at the information board at the bottom of a large stairwell informed him that the returns section was straight ahead and on the right at the end. There were two people in the queue in front of him and when his turn came he handed over some coins to settle the fine on his overdue books to a very bored looking librarian. Afterwards as he turned to come out he saw over on the left a history section and made his way through a large arch into a room with numerous shelves. At a small desk in the corner sat an elderly gentleman, one of the old school Richard thought as he noted the tweed jacket complete with bowtie. He spotted Richard and stood up. 'Good morning to you sir, is there anything in particular I can help you with today' he asked.

Richard looked at the books on the shelf in front of him and told him that anything to do with Fountains Abbey in the late 12th century and in particular the monks.

'Ah yes we have a good selection available so just give me a minute' he said as he looked at a row of books on the bottom shelf.

'Yes, I suppose it's the political side I'm particularly interested in, the appointed and the deposed'. Richard said. The old boy rummaged for a few minutes and retrieved half a dozen books that he now placed firmly in his hands.

'I think these will give you the information you are looking for' he said 'The Levens guide may be your best source of information but I'll leave you to it, if you want anything further just let me know'. Richard thanked him and found a table and chair over by a large window at the end of the room. Although he was eager to find out as much as he could he begrudged spending too much time as he wanted to get home and take his trip, Christ he was starting to sound like a junkie he thought.

The Levens guide entitled 'The Abbots of Fountains Abbey in the 12th century' proved very fruitful. He opened the cover and about three quarters of the page down the contents list spotted what he was looking for, the Abbot Linus Deyer. He turned to page 146 and there before him was a quite neat potted version of the tumultuous events over the five years that Linus was Abbott. As he read down the page he suddenly saw two names that jumped out of the page at him, the Monk Adolphus and lay-brother Conan who were both instrumental in the demise of Linus, but another piece of information that shook him even more was that Adolphus was none other than the chief bee keeper at Fountains Abbey, was this his alter ego in another time? His thoughts now raced ahead of him and he wondered if it was possible that this was him but in another time. What about those people who claimed to have been a knight of the whatever and killed in some battle or a duel with scar marks on their body that nothing else could explain. He closed his eyes and covered them with his hands to try and steady himself for a few moments. Was this Einstein's fourth dimension, the theory that time was in strands and we all walked like ghosts alongside each other. He heard a cough and looked up to see the elderly gentleman by his side. 'How are you getting on, have you found what you were looking for' he gently asked.

'Yes, yes' Richard stuttered and closed the book in front of him. 'You have been most helpful but I have to go now, other appointments' he said.

'Well I am always here and only too pleased to help, if I can' the elderly gentleman replied.

Richard was intrigued by him and asked 'How long have you been here'.

'Oh it must be about two years now, this place has been my safe haven really'. He saw Richard look at him in a puzzled way and continued. 'Yes my wife died and I couldn't face staying where we had been so happy together and as my son and his family live in Durham my course was set and I moved here two years ago'.

'I see' Richard replied. 'Can I ask what you did before'.

'I lived in Oxford and was Professor at Gabriel college teaching quantum mechanics and history, two such interesting topics and in some way so interminably linked'.

Richard now thought to himself that his elderly gentleman, that was what he now called him, was a specialist in the two fields so relevant to his situation. 'Time and history' Richard said 'and as you say so intertwined'. Richard stood up and pushed his chair back behind him, 'Just one more thing before I go, what is your name, in case I need to ask for you that is'.

'Clive, Clive Durnley' he replied ex Professor at Oxford, Phd Quantum Mech and also Phd History' he added.

Chapter Six

Richard retraced his steps out of the library and within minutes walked the last few paces to the front of No. 27 Carrow Mansions. As he opened the front gate he heard a call through the thick privet hedge that divided his property from the house next door. It was his neighbour Ted Willoughby, a nice enough chap but a bit on the talkative side for Richard.

'Hi, strange conversation I know as we can't see each other on account of the hedge but wondered if you and your good lady wife fancy coming in for a drink tonight'.

Richard's face made a small grimace as he called back 'Kind of you Ted but Susan is away this weekend and I've got some things I need to do, another time eh'. The conversation ended as he heard Ted respond with a quick o.k. as he unlocked the front door and let himself in, the house was silent. He remembered that he still had his list of chores but would have to make an excuse for them, he would say that his boss had called him with a sudden weekend request for something or another but it was now time.

Richard opened his laboratory door and walked into the small room at the back of the house. He was trying to recreate everything the same as before like some kind of ritual as he retrieved a small box from his briefcase. He hoped that the bees were still alive as he opened the lid and was pleased to hear a low buzzing sound. Now for the bit he wasn't looking forward to, the self imposed sting. With his tweezers he gently grasped one of the bees and took one last glance at it before turning his head away, his closed his eyes and clenched his teeth as he jabbed the bee into his forearm. He felt that sharp agonizing pain that lasted just seconds and was then followed by a terrible deep throbbing sensation. He now had to wait and tried to remember how long it had taken before, was it a minute, 2 minutes, whatever it was it hadn't taken long. He sat down at his desk feeling helpless and also disappointed, what if nothing happened. Looking at his watch he saw that ten minutes had now passed and nothing had changed, he turned to look out of the window behind him remembering that last time when he noticed something different things had started to happen, but the tree was still there standing completely still.

He heard a door close and thought to himself that this was it and his transportation back to the 12th century had started. He shut his eyes tight and waited a few seconds when he heard a voice shout out 'It's me darling, bloody disaster all round as Joshua has broken his leg in a rugby match'. Richard shook his head and opened his eyes, what was going on, he was still sitting in his room and it was Susan's voice he could hear coming from the hallway. He quickly removed the dead bee and tweezers from his desk and pulled his shirt sleeve down over the sting.

'I'm in the lab, I had a phone call from Brian who's panicking about this seminar next week and he wanted some more information'.

'O.k just popping upstairs to unpack my things and then we'll have a chat about tonight' she said. What about tonight he thought, God it was going from bad to worse and he just prayed that nothing happened to him now, not with Susan there.

He went into the kitchen and put the kettle on, he was so disappointed as everything had gone wrong. He heard Susan come down the stairs and turned to watch her walk through the door. 'My sister is in a terrible state, awful break apparently. It would have been the winning ball of the match when Joshua was tackled from behind and that was it. I said I would go to the hospital with her but she no just get yourself home so here I am'.

Richard remembered that she had said something about tonight and steeled himself as he said. 'You mentioned something about this evening'.

'Oh yes I nearly forgot, well on the way back I had a call from Madeline asking if we wanted to go out for a meal with her and Phillip tonight so I said yes, is that alright with you'. It wasn't really a question he thought to himself but an instruction.

Things were getting just better and better as he heard himself say 'Yes we might as well, what time' as he tried to make an effort to sound interested.

'Seven thirty for eight at Le Grand Mer, apparently Phillip has just had some kind of promotion at work so its by way of a celebration and on him too'. As it happened Le Grand Mer was a very upmarket fish restaurant and under any normal circumstances Richard would have jumped at the opportunity but not today. Going out for a meal and having to make small talk was the last thing in the world on his mind.

'Very kind of them, shall we get a cab so we can both have a drink' he said. He felt the need to anaesthetize himself and it was the only way he was going to get through tonight'.

'Yes you ring and book it for 7 o'clock and we'll get there early so we can have a nice drink together, just the two of us. I'm going up now for a long soak in the bath so we don't have to rush and it gives you plenty of time too. Don't worry about the tea you can bring me up a large gin and tonic instead'. At least Richard thought she hadn't noticed anything strange about him so that was something. He grabbed a local phone book and chose a cab service at random securing their pick up at around 7 o'clock from Carrow Mansions to Le Grand Mer in the city centre. He remembered that Susan wanted a gin and tonic and fetched some ice from the freezer. He would have to just put everything on hold for now and wondered when it would be possible to try again for another trip, it wasn't easy. Perhaps he could take himself off somewhere but would it make a difference about where it was. 'Richard have you gone to the artic for the ice' he heard Susan shout from the bathroom door.

'Yea just doing it now, the ice box is a bit frozen so I'm having to chisel it out' he replied and hoped that she wouldn't check because it was perfectly alright. Richard poured a very generous amount of gin onto the ice and heard it crackle as the alcohol melted it. A few moments later he carried her drink aloft on a tray into the bathroom much to her pleasure. 'Oh thank you darling, now I've been thinking that as it is rather a special evening what with Phillip's promotion you should wear your dark suit with a bowtie'.

Richard was a bit taken aback and asked if that was really necessary, even given the occasion, that would just round off his day now by going out for the evening looking like a bloody penguin.

'Richard please don't cross me, you must make an effort with things'. He looked down at the black and white tiles on the bathroom floor, was that an implication that he didn't he wondered.

'Fine black suit and dicky it is then' he said as he retreated through the bathroom door and back downstairs. He went to the drinks cupboard to put away the bottle of gin and spotted his Jack Daniels at the back in the corner, it was his turn now and he poured a massive tumbler full with the amber liquid and swilled it back in one go. His throat burned as he swallowed and was already reaching out for a refill. He started to think again about the idea of him getting away somewhere and doing the trip, so he wouldn't be disturbed. A plan was starting to form in his mind and it concerned the two day seminar that the Veterinary Medicines Directorate were holding next Wednesday. Brian told him that it was being held in a small town called Boroughbridge that lay only some ten miles south-east of Ripon and dare he say it, Fountains Abbey. He had put in a lot of work for this seminar and thought he wouldn't have too much trouble wangling a place for himself, yes he would put in an appearance and then he would be free in the hotel to escape. Also of course with the abbey only just up the road he would visit there as it would have been rude not to. He felt much better now that he had got some sort of plan into place and decided to ring Brian tomorrow, even though it was Sunday, and hopefully get the go ahead as it couldn't wait till Monday.

Richard looked at the bottle of Jack Daniels and saw that he had quite inadvertently drank nearly half of it, his head was starting to swim but he felt so buoyed up what with the alcohol and the plan. This evening he now thought would just go over his head and in fact he was rather starting to looking forward to it.

'The bathroom is free now, you'd better get a move on it's 6 o'clock already' he heard Susan shout.

'Yes alright, it won't take me long' he replied. Some thirty minutes later he finished tying his bow tie and admired himself in the mirror thinking to himself that he didn't look bad for 45 as he had kept both his hair and his figure. After one final brush of his hair he joined Susan downstairs just in time as he heard the front doorbell ring, their cab was now there ready and waiting for them.

CHAPTER SEVEN

Madeline and Phillip were both already there neatly sat at a table laid with a crisp white linen tablecloth. As Richard and Susan were whisked through the door with the sound of *Bon Soir* ringing in their ears their hosts stood up armed with champagne glasses and welcomed them to their table. Madeline looked resplendent in a shimmering green dress and Phillip much to Richard's relief was a penguin too.

'Such short notice I know but how pleased we are that you could make' said Madeline in a simpering voice.

'Darling we wouldn't have missed it for the world' Susan returned. A round of kissing then took place that made Richard feel quite nauseous. Phillip looked over the table at Richard and smiled 'I hear your in bees' he said.

'Yes that's right, for my sins I am employed by the BBKA also known as the British Beekeepers Association'.

'Oh and what do they do' replied Phillip.

'Quite a lot of things actually like promoting bees as a whole and the important part they play in the world's eco system, also the health of bees, that is my forte and viruses in particular. What about you and I understand that tonight is a celebration of your elevation at work' said Richard.

Phillip was fiddling with the cruet set on the table as he replied 'Me, well I bet you'd never guess, artificial limbs'.

'Your right Phillip, never in a million years. What part do you play'.

'Well first of all you'd be surprised to know exactly what a large demand there are for them, arms and legs that is. I suppose the two main causes for the demand are decease and accident and of course the recent wars in Afghanistan and Iraq have created a large demand. My part is selling them, involves a lot of hospital visits and helping to kit people out, you'd be surprised how much there is involved in it. And Madeline by way of that has ended up on the hospital board so we're quite a team. But going back to your bees, you say that your involvement is deceases' said Phillip.

'Yes, believe it or not they get ill too, even dysentery' replied Richard. He saw Susan give him a pointed look over the table.

'Richard not about as we are to eat please' she said.

'No of course not, now lets look at what delectable delights they have to tempt us tonight' said Richard. He opened the menu and cast his eyes down the starters and made his choice immediately. 'It's oysters for me' he said 'and a lot of them'.

'Yes me to, we can share a platter' said Phillip.

'Such slimy things I always think, I'm plumping for the crayfish salad' said Madeline'.

'Me too, it looks delicious' said Susan.

The waiter who had been hovering in the background now stood with his pad and pen poised. 'I have already made a note of your starters and for mains ladies and gentlemen' he enquired.

Both Susan and Madeline chose the sole Veronique, Richard the sea bass with ginger and spring onion and Phillip the stuffed sea bream with fennel sauce.

'Perfect' the waiter said as he retrieved the menus and informed them that the wine waiter would be with them in due course.

'Tell me' said Richard as he looked over at Madeline, 'what work does it involve on the hospital board'.

'Oh endless meetings and visits to these poor people after they have gone home, you just always count your blessings' she said.

'Yes' said Richard as he adjusted the cutlery in front of him. 'We all seem to live in our own little world don't we'. He thought to himself that maybe his little world wasn't that little after all, well he was here and there really, first of all in the 21st century and then back in the 12th. The arrival of the wine waiter prevented any further discussion after a muscadet for the starters was chosen and then a fine bottle of white burgundy for the ladies and a bottle of sauvignon blanc for the men, which the waiter told them would complement the dishes perfectly.

After a short while the dishes were duly delivered to the table with a fine flourish and such drama as the lids were listed off of their plates. 'I think we've chosen well' said Richard as he looked down at the half dozen oysters so plump and juicy sitting on his plate.

'Yes, bon appetite' said Phillip as he took his fork and carefully lifted one of them into his very wide mouth. 'So delicious' he mumbled. The ladies on the other side of the table daintily forked their crayfish salad adding that all was well. Silence reigned as they consumed their starters until Madeline sat back and carefully wiped her small butterfly shaped lips. 'Simply perfect' she said.

Richard was starting to feel very hot and rather unwell he admitted to himself as he wiped his brow with his serviette and ran his finger around the back of his collar. He spotted Susan eyeing him across the table 'Are you alright Richard' he heard Susan ask as she leant across the table.

'Yes I'm fine, just a bit warm. Think I will pay a visit to the gents if you will excuse me' he muttered quickly as he stood and pushed his chair behind him. 'I won't be long'.

Susan gave a long look as he disappeared from the restaurant and she apologised to the others telling them that Richard really had been working too hard lately and should take a holiday.

Richard stumbled into the gents and looked at himself in the mirror thinking to himself that he did look rather odd. Must be a dodgy oyster he thought to himself as he started to feel quite sick as he closed the door of the toilet cubicle behind him. He knelt before the toilet and started to hear a singing noise in his ears that grew louder and louder and then turned into a chant as he realised that the singing in his ears was that of a choir. As he opened his eyes he saw that the bottom of the toilet bowl had now gone and turned into the bottom of a prayer stall, the change had happened, he had gone back. It wasn't meant to be like this, why had there been this time delay unlike before when his transportation had been almost immediate. He thought of the others at the dinner table waiting for their second course while he was kneeling at mass in the 12th century.

The first thing he noticed was that it was no longer night as he lifted his eyes up and saw shafts of sunlight pouring through the huge stained glass windows, the last time it had been the same time of day but not this time. Turning to his left he saw that he was sitting at the end of a long heavily carved pew in a row of some twenty monks who were all clothed in the same greyish white woollen habits with faces that all bore the same blank expression. As he looked upward he saw the sheer splendour of the vaulted ceiling of a huge nave supported by some ten massive columns and looking again at the stained glass windows realised that he was now sitting in the church he had seen from across the other side of the cloister on his last visit. The singing had now stopped and a figure rose from a pew at the front and mounted some stairs to a pulpit at the side, he wondered if it was his abbot Linus Deyer but saw as he turned that he was a younger man clothed in purple vestments. Richard was a lapsed catholic and had been for many years, it was when his father died after a long illness with cancer that his dark night of the soul started, an expression that was used when your faith disappears and is replaced by a sense of desertion. He wondered if that was what all this was about, was he having some sort of crisis of faith and now these delusions, he shook his head what the hell was going on. As Richard looked at the fine purple vestments it did confirm one thing though, it was the holy season of lent and therefore the same time of year as back there in that other time. The priest gave a long look at the monks seated before him after which he made the sign of the cross and much to Richard's surprise found he joined the others around him in this ritual, God when was the last time he had done that he thought to himself.

'Brothers in Christ, as we enter this holy period of lent we must all search our souls and prepare for the Easter celebrations. To cleanse our minds of impure thoughts and make us ready to kneel at the cross with Christ, our dear Lord. Let us pray'.

A silence followed as the brothers all bent their heads and firmly placed their hands together and again Richard found he was following the others.

After a few moments he heard the priest clear his throat to announce the end of their private intentions and with the gesture of an arm gave them permission to sit. 'We have much to do in preparation for our Easter celebrations including I am most pleased to tell you a visit from our dear Bishop Hugh Chaloner of York. He will be with us for some four days and I know you will all do your utmost to make it a memorable and of course a holy stay'. The monks next to him quietly muttered something to each other but Richard couldn't hear what they said but guessed that the politics in life always pervaded whatever century. 'Finally we will pray for our dear brothers in the infirmary and wish them a speedy recovery'. He read out a few names and Richard remembered from the conversation he heard in the warming room that there had been a fever that had struck many of the monks including some deaths. 'In the name of the Father, Son and Holy Ghost, amen'. Richard looked up at the priest and now saw him descend the stairs from the pulpit and disappear at a side door. The monks around him now rose and started to file out of the pews and that was when he saw Adolphus some three rows behind him. He went to waive but remembered that he was invisible and silent as a ghost. He followed behind the others and walked quickly to catch up with Adolphus who was now with another monk near the door.

'Come brother Sinnulph we must make haste to the cellarium and collect the extra spices, figs and ale for our meagre Lenten rations but just think how succulent those capons will be with rice and almonds at Easter'.

They turned left and walked through a small passage that opened out into a massive undercroft some one hundred feet in length with a low rib vaulted ceiling that he found quite claustrophic. Richard thought again was it all just a delusion and remembered that next week he would be visiting here again, in his own century of course. He rummaged in his trouser pocket and found his house keys thinking they would have to do as he carved a cross and his initials RF on one of the pillars. On Tuesday he would come back and see if they were still there, that would be the conclusive proof he needed.

He heard a key turn a lock behind him and now saw Adolphus and Sinnulph enter one of the six store rooms that lay on the right hand side of the undercroft. He followed silently behind them and watched as they retrieved some sacks from a huge shelf in the corner that they put over their shoulders to carry back to the kitchen.

'Come we must hurry to the laver and make ready for dinner otherwise our bellies will be empty'.

Richard spotted some huge rounds of cheese sitting on a shelf over the far side and went for a closer look wondering exactly what type they were. Suddenly he heard a key turn in the lock and looked round to see that they had gone and he had become a prisoner shut in the store room. He quickly moved to the large wooden door and turning the handle tried to open it but it was shut fast, how had he been so silly, he should have been watching them. He started to panic and began to bang his fists on the door harder and harder, somebody would hear him. He started to shout please let me out and heard a voice the other side of the door.

'Mr Fellowes, are you alright, is the lock stuck'. How did they know his name, and as he opened his eyes saw that the wooden door had disappeared and instead he was back in the small toilet cubicle in the restaurant. Sweat was pouring down his face as he reached down and pulled the bolt back on the lock, how was he going to explain this he thought to himself. He pulled the door back to see a waiter looking at him in a puzzled way. 'Are you alright sir, it's just your party were rather concerned and said you had been feeling unwell'.

'Yes, I was but I'm o.k. now, just let me bathe my face and please tell the others I will be with them in a minute'.

'Alright sir, if you are sure that you are o.k.'.

'Yes I am thank you'. After the waiter had disappeared out the door Richard poured a huge basin of cold water and bathed his face. He looked at himself in the mirror and hoped that they wouldn't notice anything, it was just a dodgy oyster he would tell them, well seafood poisoning was a nasty thing after all. A few moments later he emerged from the gents and made his way back to a table of people with very concerned faces.

'Richard we were so worried, are you alright' Susan asked. 'We waited for a while and then asked the waiter to check the toilets'. Richard looked at the table and saw they had waited on him before their main courses.

'I'm so sorry to have spoilt the evening and the celebrations but I will have to go home, couldn't face another thing but you must have your meal' said Richard as he looked at Phillip and Madeline.

'Yes my dears, so sorry for this to have happened but I'm sure you understand' said Susan indicating to the waiter that they were going and could they please have their coats.

'Well you mustn't miss out, we'll do it again another time' said Phillip giving Richard a sympathetic look. 'You think it was one of the oysters Richard, mine were fine but it's not unusual to get a bad one, hope your soon feeling better' he added. The restaurant rang for a cab and after another flurry of apologies they disappeared out the restaurant door and into the night. In the back of the cab on their way home Susan took Richard's hand and patted it. 'Are you sure your alright, you seem to keep having these funny turns' she said. 'I wonder if the doctor should look you over'.

"No really, I was fine until I had those oysters, I won't be having them again in a hurry' he replied.

'No probably not' Susan said.

Richard looked out the window at the passing lights of other cars and the haze of the city lights disappear as they made their way back to Carrow Mansions. He wondered if Adolphus and Sinnulph had managed to deliver the provisions to the kitchen and still made it in time after all for their dinner in the refectory.

Chapter Eight

Sunday was an uneventful day and it turned out a very wet one by midday. Susan informed him that they were having roast chicken with all the trimmings and would eat at 3 o'clock as Robyn would be home by them.

Richard looked out of the sitting room window and watched rivulets of water trickle down the pane and onto the window ledge below. He thought back to his trip last night and wondered what the monks were doing now and also what the weather was like. 'Richard are you day dreaming again' said Susan as she walked into the room. 'Don't forget you're picking Robyn up at 2 o'clock and it's already half one'.

'Yes no problem, I'll just fetch my car keys and I'll be off'. He went upstairs and put on his jacket remembering that he needed to call Brian and have a chat about booking a place for himself at the two day seminar next week in Boroughbridge. After two quick telephone conversations he had not only secured his release from work as of Tuesday morning until the Friday but also a superior double room at The Mitre Head Hotel, a large establishment with conference facilities that lay on the outskirts of the town.

The only thing he now had left to do was break the news to Susan which quite frankly he wasn't looking forward to. As it happened she was quite laid back about it and said it would give her an opportunity to do her own thing next week, whatever that was he thought to himself.

The rest of the day passed without any particular note and as he sat watching some terrible comedy show on the television later that evening, he went through the programme for the following day. He would go into the office first thing and collect any papers he needed for the seminar and also of course not forgetting the vital part of the plan his apis mellefera. He would take about half a dozen with him, well he didn't really know how many trips he would be taking so best to make sure he thought. That led him on in his thoughts to the actual sting itself and its composition, were the bees with the virus different to those without? He would have to check some technical data to see if anything transpired on this point and decided that would be his first job on arriving in the office the following morning. The dreadful television programme eventually came to an end as did the evening and he went to bed that night with a feeling of excitement and great anticipation of the next few days.

He was at his desk by 9.30 a.m. with Susan's parting instructions still reverberating in his ears. Firstly he was to call her as soon as he arrived in Boroughbridge to let her know he had got there safely, make sure that he ate properly and lastly not to sit up late at night chatting. He often wondered to himself that if they had had more children would she have been different with him, he often thought he was like the surrogate child, the other one she had never had. God knows they had tried everything but it wasn't to be and they were blessed with Robyn as an only child.

George Myers had now arrived at his desk and regaled him with some boring details about his weekend that Richard was not remotely interested in. Luckily George was collared by Brian who wanted to discuss some extra duties for him in Richard's absence and he was thus left in peace.

He logged onto his computer and carefully typed in his password and clicked onto the page for bee venoms. He wanted to know if the cocktail of Apitoxin, a bitter colourless liquid with Melittin, was affected by Dicistroviridae belonging to the family Group IV also identified as a positive sense SSRNA insect infecting virus. Had the combination of these two components set of a strange chemical reaction in his body that resulted in hallucinations. Richard thought about the graffiti he had left behind on one of the columns in the cellarium and told himself that if he really had gone back in time then it would still be there tomorrow, he could hardly wait.

He looked at his watch and saw that it was already midday and at that moment in time made a pact with himself, that if tomorrow's visit to the cellarium proved fruitless and the column was devoid of any marking then he would cease any more of his trips, however, and here he took a deep inward breath, if his initials were there then he would pursue this to the bitter end, whatever that might prove to be. Any further thoughts were interrupted as he was suddenly aware of someone standing the other side of his desk peering down at him and looked up to meet the steady gaze of Piers Marchmont, the Associate Director of the BBKA and his ultimate boss. He was a tall imposing figure with a tidy moustache and a smart head of dark black hair. It was rumoured that in his younger days he was in the SAS but it was something always left to conjecture.

'My you look busy Richard, if all my staff were as conscientious as you I would die a happy man'.

Richard shut his screen down and shuffled some papers together on his desk, 'Yes I'm just making sure that I've got everything I need for the seminar'.

'I'll be arriving late tomorrow night Richard so I thought we could have breakfast together on Wednesday morning'.

'Yes I'll look forward to it' Richard replied. 'I'm actually going to Boroughbridge this afternoon so I can give a hand tomorrow, with setting up for Wednesday' he added.

'Yes well done, so I'll see you Wednesday' Piers said as he walked out of the door.

Richard would have liked more time to look at this apitoxin theory and the possible link to dicistroviridae but left it there. He needed to make a quick visit to the laboratory to collect a small supply of apis mellafera and then he would be on his way. He felt elated and quite light headed at the prospect of it all, he felt like some elicit lover off to a clandestine affair except that with him it wasn't a woman but the 12th century.

The journey only took about two hours as he quickly sailed down the M1 that eventually led to the A1 and at 4 o'clock pulled into the large car park at The Mitre Head hotel on the outskirts of Boroughbridge. At the reception desk he was checked in by a very clinical looking woman who hurried through the registration with him as soon as possible. Richard looked around the foyer while his details were entered on the computer and a room key retrieved from a large board behind the desk. These sort of hotels could not hold a candle to the older ones he thought, everything was all the same whether you were in this town or that town. The shops were all the same too he thought and concluded that that was globalisation for you.

'Your keys Mr Fellows' he heard a voice say. 'Some of your party are here already and over in the conference centre' she added.

Richard wanted to steer well clear of the others, get to his room unpack and make the most of his solitude and the opportunity that it would afford him to trip. He soon found his room located on the ground floor at the back of the hotel at the opposite end to the conference facilities and well out of the way much to his delight. He unlocked the door and saw before him a characterless room with a bathroom just off to the right and a window that looked out onto the car park at the back, perfect he thought. He threw his holdall onto the bed quickly unpacking his night clothes and hanged the remainder of its contents in the wardrobe. Lastly he carefully put his case containing the bees onto a corner shelf and undid the catches slowly raising the lid. He heard the comforting hum of the bees and knew that everything was ready. It was 5 o'clock and after a quick phone call to Susan to confirm his safe arrival at the hotel he had no commitments to anyone other than the 12th century.

He went through the same painful ordeal as he closed his eyes and jabbed the bee into his forearm and that awful sensation that fortunately lasted only seconds and was then replaced by a deep throbbing sensation. He sat on a chair by the window and waited quietly for something to happen as he noticed two people walking across the car park towards the hotel and then saw the transformation happen that unlike before was now so distinct and clear. The numerous cars and dark tarmac beneath them disappeared and replaced by the solid dark green of a square cloister lawn and the two figures previously dressed in suits were now in long white robes complete with shaven heads, he had gone back.

Richard looked around him and saw that there were two windows and a door facing out onto the cloister and the church with its huge stained glass windows was now on his right. As he looked left he noticed three different buildings and worked out that the nearest one must be where he had arrived back on his first visit. It had to be the warming house as it was the only room in the monastery except for the kitchens and infirmaries where a fire was kept burning during the winter months so that the monks could restore circulation to their frozen limbs after hours spent in the cold of the cloister and the church. Also it was used for the bleeding of monks as he recalled the barbaric scene he had witnessed that day. The middle building had the most huge impressive arched doorway with some kind of washing facility on either side with a long wash-basin supported on a stone bench, this was surely the laver that Adolphus had referred to that day in the cellarium that they needed to get back to in order to prepare themselves for their meal in the refectory. Turning now Richard looked around the inside of the room that had another tall vaulted ceiling and four columns carved with the most intricate foliage, a stone platform in three tiers against the side walls gave the appearance of some kind of seating arrangement and at the far end sat a large chair in a huge niche that held place of honour.

He heard a latch open and turning watched as the two figures from the car park, it was so confusing he meant cloister, come into the room. They were neither old nor young and emanated a certain superiority Richard thought.

'I can't think why we have been summoned before the others' said one of them 'Our day will be delayed now with a late chapter-mass' he added.

'You should worry William I have been up since midnight preparing for the nightly vigil, that reminds me prior Heribert is meant to be here too but is no doubt instructing the young sub-prior on his duties, he has to be reminded of everything and even ringing the dorter bell it seems'.

The door opened and a tall thin man now entered the room and looked enquiringly at the others 'So why have we been called, what is this about?'.

Before a reply could be given the door opened once more and the trio bowed their heads, this must be the Abbot Linus Deyer Richard thought to himself as he bade them sit down and then took his seat at the far end of the room. He remembered on his first trip that Adolphus and Conan had described him as an older man which he certainly was and also a very worried looking one at that. There was a slight pause as the Abbot looked at each of them in turn and cleared his throat.

'Prior Robert Heribert, Cellarer William Jerome and Sacrist Henry Gower, all my loyal men I trust but today I must speak to you of financial problems, a huge debt'. He closed his eyes and placed his hands together as if in prayer. 'I am being pulled from all sides it seems with taxes and loans imposed by our pope, not to mention the king's constant demands for supplies for his wars and expeditions. You each have an obedientiary held in your own trust and it is that to which I must now refer'.

'We are not trusted then Abbott' said William Jerome who now rose to his feet and approached the huge chair at the end of the room.

'Please do not be offended, I am only following a course of action that hopefully will restore some substance to our finances' said the Abbot.

'Are we too under suspicion' asked Robert Heribert and Henry Gower waiting anxiously for the Abbot's response.

The Abbot shook his head in a desolate fashion 'No one is under suspicion, I am only trying to make some sort of sense of things, please bear with me brothers. I am considering appointing a bursar but believe that it will only lead to further confusion so I ask that you each present your own financial scripts. The Bishop is arriving on Thursday for the start of our Easter celebrations, while he is here I hope to allay his fears of which I have unfortunately heard much about already notwithstanding those of the King as well'.

Richard looked at William Jerome and noted a certain glint in his eyes, he wasn't sure if it was anger or pure fear but something was amiss.

'Have it your own way Abbot, as soon as mass is over I will make a start' said William. He looked over at the others 'You must do the same brothers and we will be ready to celebrate Easter with a clear head'.

Richard heard the steady toll of a large bell and looked out of the window and watched as a number of monks approached the door, it was the bell summoning them to mass. The bell now sounded different and as he looked out saw the cloister green disappear and the car park replace it. The bell he now heard was the telephone ringing in his bedroom, he had gone back to his own time. He walked over and lifting the receiver was told by a calm reassuring voice at the other end of the line that his alarm call was booked and he would be rung at 8 o'clock the following morning.

CHAPTER NINE

Richard was up had breakfast and on the road by 9 o'clock. It was a bright sunny day that promised a warm spring afternoon and within twenty minutes he sailed through the small village of Marton-le-Moor. A local sign post reliably informed him that he was only four miles east of Ripon and the B6265 would take him through the centre of the cathedral city and famous market town.

About an hour later he approached Fountains and obediently followed a sign to the western car park. A short walk took him through the outer court past Fountains Hall, a magnificent Jacobean mansion built in 1598 with stone from the Abbey ruins. The style of the building was attributed to the Elizabethan architect Robert Smythson. It had an extremely impressive façade with symmetrical lawns at the front that were flanked by topiary elephants. As he approached the gatehouse he looked at the west front of the abbey church and on its right a vast length of the west range of claustral buildings. This would not have been the view of any medieval visitor as high walls would have hid the line of cellarer's buildings that lay behind. He had taken the opportunity of obtaining a copy of the guide book for the abbey beforehand and read about what things had looked like, not forgetting of course that some of them he had already seen with his own eyes.

At the ticket office he purchased a ticket and joined a small group of people who were already waiting for the National Trust guide to take them around the abbey. He kicked his heels in the gravel underfoot and looked at the others who were a mixed bunch. There was an elderly couple complete with umbrellas and walking sticks, a young couple who were obviously more interested in each other than anything else, a young mother and her son who was already complaining and starting to whine and a very well dressed middle aged couple. He overhead their conversation and detected an american drawl as the woman told her husband how lucky these English people were to have such old buildings. As he looked at them she turned round and smiled 'We have nothing like this back home of course, our oldest buildings are only a couple of hundred years.'. She extended her hand to Richard 'Marge McClusky and this is my husband Gerry, from Detroit' she added.

'Yes I heard your accent but you have a Scottish surname' Richard said.

'Oh people always ask about that, well the truth of it is that my husband's ancestors were at Colludon, one of those brave men in a kilt brandishing a sword or whatever it was they used' said Marge.

'Don't believe everything she tells you, I think that it's just one of her flights of fancy and also of course wanting to be just a tiny part of your history' said her husband.

Richard smiled and nodded his head 'Well as far as I know none of my ancestors were at Culloden, I'm from the South but now living up north because of my work'. He guessed what the next question would be and beat them to it as he added that he worked for the BBKA and was involved in researching bee viruses.

'How interesting' Gerry replied but any further conversation was prevented as their guide had now arrived and started shepherding them together. He was a young man with a cherry smile dressed in the National Trust uniform complete with umbrella that he now put up and raised above his head.

'Good morning to everyone my name is Adam and welcome to Fountains Abbey, the showcase of Cistercian monks. When they first arrived in this valley in 1132 and a bitter cold winter, they sheltered under rocks at the side of the dale and then built a hut beneath a great elm tree near the eastern end of the present precinct. In 1133 they started to erect timber buildings and in 1135 more permanent buildings with stonework were constructed.

'Oh my' said Marge, just think of those poor monks in that freezing weather wearing nothing more than woollen habits'.

Adam smiled and said 'Yes but in those days human beings were more hardy, we have all been so cosseted in the 21st century with central heating and wall to wall carpeting'.

'Still sounds like some kind of hell to me' Marge replied.

'Yes well we must start our tour of this magnificent setting and will commence with the abbey and work our way round' said Adam 'If you have any questions please just ask me and I will do my best to answer them. If you lag behind at any time just look for my striped umbrella' he said now raising it up and down above his head.

The group followed Adam into the Great Court and stopped at the front part of the church. 'The place was called Fountains, where, at that time and afterwards so many drank of waters springing up to eternal life as from the fountains of the Saviour. These were the immortal words of William of Newburgh a twelfth-century Augustian canon' said Adam. 'Its beginnings were inauspicious but it became the largest and richest of the Northern abbeys. Fountains stemmed from the Benedictine house of St. Mary's of York where a group of reform-minded monks fled from their abbey to pursue a harsher and more disciplined way of monastic life'. He pointed to the ruined porch cover and reliably informed them that this was the Galilee porch as they walked through into the nave of the mighty church. Once assembled inside the entrance Adam pointed up to a great Perpendicular window above the central doorway and informed them that this one of seven lights inserted by Abbot Darnton in the year before his death.

Richard looked around and saw at once how different it looked to that last time when he had sat at mass in one of the pews further up the nave which had then been divided by a series of screens but was now an open expanse. He concluded that a change in their ritual arrangements would have been the main reason for this difference but noted that the rood screen and its altar had still been retained. He now heard the scream of a rook as it flew through one of the huge eyeless windows above him and he looked up and saw the pale blue sky through the open roof overhead.

'On the left in the north transept a perpendicular tower was constructed by Abbot Marmaduke Huby between 1495 and 1526. It is divided by internal floors into five storeys and the design of the windows varies on each storey, the ground and third floor windows have two-centred heads, the first floor four-centred or elliptical heads and the top floor flat heads. Bands of inscription are placed beneath the embattled parapet and beneath the two upper tiers of windows. The Latin texts are taken from the Cistercian breviary and include the verse from the first epistle to Timothy. *Regi autem secularism immortali; invisibili, soli Deo, honor et gloria in saecula secularism.* Now unto the King eternal, immortal, invisible, the only God, be honour and glory forever and ever'.

The group fell silent as they walked around and gazed up in awe at the huge tower above them. 'The top of the tower was designed to have large pinnacles at each angle, standing out on the face of the buttresses and connected to the parapet by miniature flying buttresses with a smaller pinnacle set diagonally and corbelled out from the parapet in the middle of each side. In addition to the inscriptions the external faces of the tower have niches set above seven of the windows, some of which still contain their statues'. Adam had been trained to give his visitors space, that was what they called it, to observe and absorb and that was what he now did. He noticed Richard who seemed in comparison with the others to be particularly interested in his guided tour and he wandered over to him now. 'Do you have any particular interest, is it work or otherwise' Adam enquired.

'Oh just an interest that's all' replied Richard who thought to himself that the otherwise didn't bear thinking about and indeed if he revealed his true intentions the guide would surely think he was mad. 'It's just the amazing feat of constructing this edifice with such primitive means, I'm sure there were many fatalities' said Richard.

'Yes that's true, it was done with nothing more than pulleys and ropes, no cranes or hydraulics then' said Adam. He glanced at his wrist watch and informed the group that it was time to move on and a short walk would take them through the Infirmary by the River Skell to the Fountains elm and approximate birthplace of the abbey.

'I will leave you here' said Richard who had his own itinerary and that was through the passage out of the South Transept and into the cloister that would lead him to the buildings that were of particular interest to him.

Richard waived his arm and wished him well as he heard his voice disappear into the background telling them that the Infirmary was part of the abbey where the sick and aged received treatment in an area that was removed from the noise and bustle of the great court.

Richard walked through a passage and out onto the cloister remembering his first sight of it from the warming house only a few days ago. If he was right the Chapter House would be the first on his left and after a few paces he stopped at an entrance. Looking through he immediately recognised what was left of the room, albeit now without a roof and much of it gone and saw the three tiers against the walls and the niche where the abbot's chair had stood. The main difference though was that the entrance he had now walked through was set further back onto the cloister with a vestibule and the northern and southern compartments were walled off as book cupboards that could be entered from the cloister by two arches on either side. The conversation he had heard that day went round in his head, the Abbot had smelt a rat and a very large one at that. He was now being pressurized by the Bishop and had even heard rumblings from the King. He wondered what would happen and hoped fervently that he would have the opportunity to find out first hand.

Richard took one last look before returning to the cloister and a few paces took him to the remains of the first entrance on the south side of the cloister and what he knew would be the warming room. He peered in and immediately saw on the left at the far end the remains of a massive fireplace, it was of course the first thing he had seen that night when it had all started. It no longer had a deep red glow but was crumbling after being made redundant for the last five hundred years after Henry VIII's actions and the dissolution of the monasteries. The two figures he had seen by the fire, Adolphus and Conan, were long since dust as well as the monks over in the corner who he had watched perform their ancient ritual of blood letting. Richard felt depressed when he thought about turning to nothing but dust and the end to which we would all come eventually. He wondered what it was that made life meaningful, could it be said that death in its own way was what made life meaningful and not meaningless. He took one last look and his thoughts turned now to the jewel in the crown, the cellarium and his graffiti.

Out on the cloister his footsteps took him past the lavers he had seen from the chapter house window. They were now empty and dry with massive chunks of masonry missing, long since released from their utilitarian purpose. He thought of the Fraterer whose duty it would have been to remove any dirt or dregs lying in the bottom of it so that the brethren would have clean water to wash their hands and faces before entering the refectory. He looked over and saw an entrance just off the end of the walkway that he knew would take him into the cellarium and he paused slightly before walking over the huge stone doorstep. It really hadn't changed that much and still possessed that overpowering claustophobic feeling he had been aware of on his last visit. The store rooms at the side where he had been locked in had now gone and were just part of the general open space. The moment had come, he nervously walked towards the pillar where he had carved his name, he had chosen the one adjacent to the entrance to avoid any confusion when he went back. He briefly closed his eyes and then opened them, there it was now greatly disfigured with the ravages of time but just about visible to the human eye, RF with a cross through the middle, he had been there.

CHAPTER TEN

When Richard arrived back at the Great Court he spotted the striped umbrella of the guide still held aloft and Adam's voice informing them that the official tour was now over and that if they wanted tea it was being served in the café over the other side of the entrance. Marge spotted Richard and called out to him 'You have missed such a treat, how interesting and such a sobering moment looking at the site of the elm tree where it had all began. Perhaps you would care to join us for tea, I can't wait to try this parkin cake I have heard so much about'.

'Very kind of you but I have an appointment' replied Richard, he wanted to get back to the hotel and another sting, time was short and there was much to do. He bade them farewell and within minutes was behind the wheel of his car and pulling out of the car park back on the road to the Mitre Head Hotel. He put his foot down and within the hour pulled into the hotel carpark and went in through the back entrance as he wanted to avoid meeting any of the seminar group. A flashing light on the telephone extension back in his room told him that somebody had tried to contact him and left a message. He picked up the receiver and pressed key 9 to hear Susan's voice at the other end of the line. She hoped he was alright and being obedient, eating his meals and not sitting up late at night. He put the receiver back in its cradle and realised he was starving hungry as after a very early breakfast he had eaten nothing all day. Perhaps he should have taken up Marge's offer of afternoon tea but then maybe not he thought to himself. He saw a menu propped up on a shelf above the phone and rang room service to order a chicken burger with salad and a plate of chips. A bright voice at the other end of the line told him that his order was placed and would be with him in the next 45 minutes.

He now repeated what had become such a painful experience of jabbing the bee into his forearm and the few seconds of searing pain that followed. He thought to himself that he must buy some more long sleeved tops as his arms were starting to represent those of a junky with their nasty perforations and scabs. He felt tired after such an early start and laid down on the bed while he waited for something to happen. He wasn't sure if he had fallen asleep but when he opened his eyes he no longer saw the plain bare walls of his room at the Mitre Head Hotel but the dark grey colour of heavy stone walls instead. There was a colourful tapestry covering on one side embroidered with the unmistakable story of the Garden of Eden with Adam and Eve and the forbidden fruit from the tree. He heard voices and raised himself on one arm to look around. It was a small room some ten feet by twelve feet and furnished in a Spartan manner with just a chair and a small altar in one corner. He lifted his legs off the bed and padded quietly to a door in the corner from where the sound of voices had come. He pulled the door back slowly and saw a large outer room before him with two figures sitting by a window. He recognised the Abbot immediately and another figure he had not seen before dressed in fine vestments with a mitre on his head, this must surely be the Bishop Hugh Chaloner Richard thought. He could not hear what they were saying as they spoke in a quiet almost conspiritorial tone so Richard as before moved like a ghost and stood beside them, they totally unaware of his presence.

'Abbott what news have you from your obedientiaries as I know you were to question them about their business' said the Bishop.

The Abbott drew a deep breath and placed his hands together in his lap 'I have summoned them and explained the dire situation we are placed in and asked them to present me with their findings, it will take longer than I had hoped with all the Easter commitments but I will let you have word as soon as I can' he said. The Abbott thought about his meeting with them in the Chapter House and hated to admit it but had doubts about their honesty. Certain things had happened that needed to be explained and although Richard had not seen it the Abbott too had spotted a certain glint in the eyes of William Jerome.

'I don't need to tell you as I am sure you already know that Henry II is most displeased', the Bishop fell silent for a few seconds and continued 'And I also have it on good authority that our Pope Lucius III is none too happy either'.

A silence hung in the air until the Bishop cleared his throat and rose from his chair to look out of the window. 'I find it somewhat ironical that so much debt is placed on us from the King with his crusades and I, yes I am somehow to blame. What about the endless hospitality that is enjoyed by the royal court and nobles, this will all have to be curtailed of that there is no question'. He raised his hands in the air and left it as an unanswered question.

'No doubt Abbott but we must all do the best we can'.

A bell tolled in the background and the Bishop watched as the quiet of the cloister area was broken by the arrival of a large numbers of monks who spilled out onto the inner square green through various doors and alleyways making their way to the entrance of the refectory.

'Come Bishop we must eat now, the Kitchener will be providing us with some tasty morsels today as part of our Easter fest'.

The Bishop stood and kissed the Abbott on both cheeks and patted his shoulder 'Before we join the brethren we must first pray in the chapel'.

The Abbot nodded his head in agreement and Richard followed close behind them through a door and down some stairs into a long passage leading out onto the cloister. He got his bearings and realised they had come from a building that lay South of the Chapter House meaning it was the Abbot's quarters. They walked past the Chapter House and turned right into a small passage and then through an entrance. Richard's sense of bearings told him that they were now at the South transept of the church but something had caught his eye and he followed them no further. He saw above him what was an unmistakable beehive, unlike anything he had ever seen before carved into the stonework on the pinnacles of the roof, a man-made stone hive. In the centre was an intricately carved stone flower and he was mesmerised as it seemed to him that just for his benefit a number of bees were now flying in and out of the carved entrance. He had of course read about the famous discovery of two beehives at Rosslyn Chapel but never actually expected to see one. This would be Adolphus' workplace Richard thought to himself, where the honey was made and collected by him, the custos apium. He wondered how many of the other monks were involved, the melittarii, those involved in beekeeping but as always so many unanswered questions. What he really needed he thought to himself was more time, his visits were always so short it seemed. What was he saying Richard thought to himself, if he could make a permanent transition would he? Of course he knew the answer to that but just wished he had more control over the length of his trips. If the amount of sting was increased would the volume of time increase, he decided it was worth a go and would try it out on another trip.

He quickly stepped to one side as he heard footsteps and watched the Bishop and Abbot emerge from the chapel and Richard as always it seemed obediently followed them back into the cloister and towards the refectory. At the lavers they both washed their hands and faces while the Fraterer dutifully handed them towels to dry themselves afterwards. Richard went to wash as well and then drew his hands back, what was he doing he thought to himself, all too often it seemed he confused the past with the present. He looked down at his body that was totally visible to him but invisible to all those around him.

In the refectory long heavy wooden trestle tables were laid with crude eating implements and mugs where the monks now sat happily chatting to their table companions. The tables groaned with some of the most delicious food Richard had ever seen. Down the middle were large serving platters with vegetables, meat puddings, eggs, some kind of game, fish, beef, mutton and last but not least the capons with rice and almonds that Adolphus had spoke about so lovingly that day in the storeroom. Some jugs were now placed at various intervals on the tables and everything was complete.

As the Bishop and the Abbot entered the refectory the brethren fell totally silent as any conversation now was a punishable offence and rewarded with bread and water and after such a lengthy period of lent nothing would keep them from the feast they were about to commence. Richard watched as the Bishop and Abbot made their way to a raised platform on the south wall of the refectory that was broader and higher than the others and obviously where the hierarchy of the abbey sat for their meals. The refectory was a noble looking room measuring some 47 feet across by 110 feet in length and divided into two aisles by four columns. The quick movement of a figure out of the corner of Richard's eye caught his attention as he watched one of the monks disappear through a small doorway and reappear a few moments later on a pulpit higher up on the right hand side of the refectory wall. The Bishop stood up and made the sign of the cross and muttered a quiet prayer to the other monks who all now stood with their heads bowed. After they sat down the monk in the pulpit read a verse from the Bible, it was in fact the monk informed them a reading from the gospel of John and told how Christ was reunited with his disciples after his resurrection.

Richard's mouth began to water at the sight of all the food and such glorious aromas that he found himself sitting at the table and started to help himself to some of the food. This was Easter Sunday he thought to himself, a day of celebration. He reached over and spooned some of the fish and capon, not forgetting the rice with almonds onto his plate and began to fork it into his mouth. The taste he was so looking forward to was nothing like he imagined because as he looked down at his plate he no longer saw those delectable morsels but a chicken burger and salad instead. He chewed the stale chicken and bun as if it were sawdust, the transition had happened as quickly as that, he had returned to the present day and already collected his room service meal on a tray from outside his bedroom door and was sitting on his bed. The meal was long cold and he calculated that he had put the order in around 4.30 pm and therefore it must have been delivered around 5.15 p.m. A glance at his watch told him that the time was now 9 o'clock so that was some three hours ago. He thought back to his trip and reckoned that he was there for no more than an hour or so at most, the time difference was strange and it passed much slower than here in the present day. He put the tray down and thought to himself that he did not have the stomach for this meal, in fact he thought to himself he didn't seem to have the stomach much for anything else either.

CHAPTER ELEVEN

Richard quickly showered and changed his shirt and trousers thinking to himself that he best put in an appearance as the others would start to wonder where he was. He glanced in the long mirror on the wall before he left as he felt anxious sometimes that he may look different in some way and didn't want to arouse any suspicion.

Back in the reception area he was informed that the Coronation Bar was the third on the right and as he neared the door heard raucous laughter coming from inside. Walking through the door he immediately recognised some of the people from the Veterinary Medicines Directorate he had met before, Tom Maitland, John Pendlebury and Roger Day.

'Hi Richard over here' said Tom 'We were beginning to wonder where you were'.

Richard shook the hand now extended to him by Roger and smiled 'Yes I got here yesterday and been doing some catching up with my reading for tomorrow'.

'That's fortunate' said Tom 'We'll be wanting you to say a few words in the seminar tomorrow, we want to hear all about your latest findings on this KBV'.

Richard swallowed as he had been doing nothing of the kind and swore quietly under his breath. 'Yes, yes, no problem, what time am I on' he enquired.

'Well we're kicking off at 10 o'clock so probably early in the afternoon session, if that's alright with you' said Tom.

Richard was looking forward to turning in early but now had visions of burning a lot of midnight oil in order to put something together. 'Fine I hope you find it of interest' he said.

'Who wants a drink' said Richard now moving towards the bar to place his order deciding that he needed one and a very large one at that.

'Of course the general public just don't realise the implications of this massive decline in our bee population' said Tom. 'They think it's just part of the big eco trip but of course that's not the case at all'.

'Well I think the more they hear about it the sooner people are going to realise there is a situation, a very serious one at that and liken it to the future when wars will be waged over water supplies' said John.

Richard returned from the bar and handed the drinks round to the others. 'Of course a most interesting source of the origins of bee keeping can be found in the Domesday Book written a hundred years ago' he said.

The others fell silent and now looked at him in astonishment. 'Surely you mean nearly a thousand years ago' said Roger.

Richard realised what he had said and felt his face colour, it had happened again this confusion between the past and the present. 'Yes, yes' he stuttered 'I mean a thousand years ago'. There was now an awkward silence and to cover it up Richard quickly continued. 'Reference was made in the Domesday Book to beekeeping equipment in

Herefordshire and the *vascular*, a small hive probably made of wicker. *Vasa apum* is also used to describe the hives in Huntingdonshire and other eastern counties. The term *rusca* was used to describe the wicker hives possibly covered with tree bark in Suffolk. The earliest archaeological evidence of the types of hives noted in the Domesday include the remains of a coiled straw skep from Coppergate dating back to the twelfth century.

'My you are quite a mine of information on the history of beekeeping' said Tom. 'Perhaps you can include some of these interesting facts in your talk tomorrow'.

Richard straightened his tie and congratulated himself on how he had got out of that one quite easily by blinding them with facts remembered from all those years ago when he learnt parrot fashion for an exam that had led to his present position at the BBKA. 'I'm glad that you find it as interesting as I do, after all from such meagre beginnings etc. etc.'.

He heard someone call his name and turned round to see Piers Marchmont appear through the bar door. 'I guessed you would all be here in the watering hole' said Piers as he now shook hands enthusiastically with them all. 'Didn't think I would make it here this early but due to a cancelled appointment and light traffic, well here I am'.

'We've just been having the most interesting conversation with Richard and for some reason or another he thought the Domesday Book was written only a hundred years ago' said Tom.

'Oh, you've been here that long' said Piers looking at Richard. 'Don't drink too much of that stuff or otherwise you'll be good for nothing tomorrow and I understand you are on first thing in the afternoon'.

'Yes' said Richard as he suppressed the feeling that he would liked to have throttled Tom. 'I thought that I would go through the whole gamut, from those humble beginnings to where we are now' he said.

An hour passed in idle chatter until Richard excused himself saying he had to ring Susan and brush up on his notes for tomorrow. As he walked out of the bar he heard Piers remind him that they were having breakfast tomorrow and he would meet him in the reception at 8 o'clock.

'Yes looking forward to it' said Richard over his shoulder as he exited and made the way back to his room. He threw his jacket off and loosened his tie, what a bloody evening and thought to himself that maybe this idea of coming to the seminar was not such a good one after all. He could have gone to Fountains Abbey anyway on the pretext of a business visit, but instead he was here being picked up on things by the delightful Tom Maitland and into the bargain now had to give a presentation tomorrow afternoon.

He sat on the bed and put his head in his hands, he was just tired he thought and after a quick call to Susan he would go to bed. He then remembered about his speech tomorrow and decided that he knew enough to put something together and talk off the top of his head and keep it short, very short and sweet he thought to himself.

Chapter Twelve

In the Coronet restaurant Richard looked over the breakfast table at Piers who had his head stuck in a newspaper and apart from the occasional mutterings of approval or disapproval about some article or another silence prevailed. Richard scooped up the last part of his scrambled egg that was rather good as it happened and drained his coffee cup.

'Portofino' said Piers as he lowered his newspaper and stared at Richard.

'Pardon' Richard replied now eyeing his table companion.

'Portofino, Rosemary and I have always dreamed of going there. We can fly to Genoa and then hire a car. We can motor round the Italian Riviera first and then travel on to the French Riviera and visit all those dazzling spots, Monaco, Monte Carlo, Cannes and of course Nice famous for its flower market. I understand that it still looks exactly the same as it did in that famous film with Grace Kelly and Cary Grant, To Catch a Thief. You've seen the film I take it and of course the ultimate irony is that Grace Kelly died in that terrible car accident driving around the bends in the mountain, it was a replica of a scene in the film when they were making an escape from their pursuers. Do you believe in fate Richard'.

Richard thought about fate, did he believe in it. Was it his fate that he should somehow return to the 12th century and if so why. He shook his head and replied 'Fate, a belief of the Greek philosopher Epicurus, I really couldn't say Piers'. Richard turned his thoughts to the Lake District, that is where he would like to have gone on holiday but unfortunately he was outnumbered in that Susan and Robyn would prefer an idyllic beach with lots of sunshine and nothing to do.

'I've never been to the Riviera in Italy or France but heard that it's very beautiful' replied Richard.

'Well it's our 30th wedding anniversary in the summer so I think we'll celebrate in style, Rosemary will be over the moon'.

Holidays Richard thought to himself, of course the word originally came not surprisingly from Holy Day, the day that people worshipped a feast day on the holy calendar, when those pilgrims walked or even on donkeys made their way across North West Spain to the Santiago de Compostela, the capital of Galicia to worship the bones of St James. He thought that if his monks could go on holiday that was where they would go. Now in our secular society the word conjured up images of cheap beach holidays or luxury cruises.

'Richard what are you thinking about' said Piers who had now put his paper down and was staring at him intently.

'Oh nothing really, just about the origin of holidays' he replied.

'You're all set for this afternoon I hope' said Piers. 'I know that there is a lot of interest in your talk and people are really looking forward to it. Apparently they are filming the whole of the proceedings so best bib and tucker'.

'Yes' Richard replied obediently.

'Well I think as I have a free morning so to speak I'm going to get on that internet and start planning the Grand Rivera Tour. I can smell that sea and sand already' he said now standing up and sliding his newspaper under his arm. See you at 2 'o clock in the conference room'.

Richard watched Piers disappear out of the dining room and glanced at his watch. It was 10 o'clock and he had four hours to go before his presentation. He briefly toyed with the idea of taking a trip but decided against it as he had no control over the time factor involved. He felt like getting some fresh air and decided that a walk round Boroughbridge might be rather nice. When he had arrived and driven through the small town he spotted a selection of antique and bric-a-bac shops and wondered if he might find a small gift for Susan. Also he had seen a very traditional cafe and thought that he would round it of with a nice cup of coffee that he knew would be served in an old style cup and saucer as opposed to the usual heavy china mug.

Some three hours later and some £150.00 lighter Richard adjusted his bow tie in the mirror. He glanced down at the box on his bed that contained a very beautiful bedside lamp, the owner of the antique shop had reassured him that it was late Edwardian and he had got a bargain at the price. Richard wasn't too sure about that but was very pleased none the less as he knew that it would placate Susan to some extent, she was so keen to get the house straight and regularly reminded him about the decorating that needed attention.

He picked up the notes for his talk that were nothing more than bullet points, each reminding him of some salient point that he would need to relay to the expectant throng. He would start off by informing them of his role at the BBKA and in particular his research about the Kashmir Bee Virus. Then he would delve into the history of bee keeping and finish with a flurry on the plight of the bee and its future, the *raison d'etre* in fact of the seminar, all quite neat he thought to himself. He looked once more in the mirror before leaving his room and thought to himself with some satisfaction you'll do, in fact you'll do very nicely.

CHAPTER THIRTEEN

Richard licked his lips and admitted to himself that he felt quite nervous as it happened but acknowledged that that was no bad thing and thus as a result so many people gave their best performance. He glanced to his left on the podium and recognised most of the faces from the Veterinary Medicines Directorate including that of Tom Maitland and he gave an inward shudder, he really didn't like that man and in particular after his chosen comments in the bar last night. Turning to his immediate right was Piers Marchmont and a few lesser mortals from the BBKA who had been pulled in at the last minute.

'Are you alright' said Piers briefly touching Richard's arm 'You'll be fine'.

Richard managed a wry smile and nodded as the hall fell silent and Professor George Applewhite, head of the Veterinary Medicines Directorate and also affectionately known as Bumble on account of his absolute devotion to bees, now stood up and gave a small bow making his way to the microphone. He cleared his throat and welcomed everyone to the seminar and hoped that it would be a most fruitful as well as a most enjoyable experience for everyone.

He turned and with a small gesture introduced Richard Fellowes, the young and rising star from the BBKA who would now address them.

A thunderous sound of clapping now filled the hall and Richard made his way to the microphone. He let the applause die down and continued, 'I am most honoured to be here today and like all of us have bees at the centre of our hearts, our future and our rock on which so much depends'. Piers behind him nodded enthusiastically and waited for Richard to continue. 'It seems only yesterday that I made that decision as a young graduate to pursue bees, but I did and here I am today'. He paused and remembering his bullet points went on to elaborate about his role at the BBKA and after a short while came to the part that he was most looking forward to, the history of bee keeping. 'You may or may not have heard of several books on husbandry written in the 1200's called "*Ceo est hosebonderie*", albeit by an unknown author on the practices of bee keeping. That each hive of bees ought to give every year for two hives on the average, for some give none, and others give three or four times a year. In some places they are given nothing at all to eat in the winter, and in some they are fed; and where they are fed it is possible to maintain eight hives right through the winter on a gallon of honey; and if you collect the honey every other year, you would have two gallons of honey from each hive". He paused slightly and continued. 'Another important work of the time was "*De Naturis Rerum*" an encyclopedia of learning by Alexander Neckham who said that bees supply us with moral lessons; they begin life as legless grubs and finally rise to the possession of wings, they are chaste, obedient to their King, and have all things in common—they are in fact typical monks'. He paused slightly to draw breath. 'Yesterday I took the opportunity of visiting Fountains Abbey the UK's largest monastic ruin and a World Heritage site that I'm sure some of you may already know, the jewel in the crown of the Cisterican order, the white monks. They arrived in the Skell Valley in the early 1200's and from such humble beginnings great things came. The monks were mostly known for their sheep farming, the wool' he added 'But also and perhaps not so well known bees, black bees to be precise.

Piers sitting behind him had began to wonder where Richard was going with his talk but now nodded gently, Richard always pulled something out of the bag, he was never boring and knew how to tell a good story although where this one was going he wasn't too sure.

'They sometimes say that the past is our key to the future, that maybe we can reverse the decline in the UK's honeybee population by commencing a breeding programme with the black bees that would increase the number of native colonies and hopefully reduce the dramatic losses in recent years'. The hall was totally silent as they hung on his every word. 'The black honeybee has thick black hair and a larger body to help keep it warm in a cooler climate plus a shorter breeding season to reflect our English summer. When I was at Fountains yesterday I saw for myself these bees flying in out of a most intricately carved stone flower from the pinnacle of a man-made stone hive set in the roof of the church in the South transept'.

There were some confused faces now in the audience and a total silence as they stared at Richard.

'Adolphus is the chief bee keeper at Fountains, I have yet to meet him but when that occasion arises I will have the opportunity to discuss this breeding programme with him'. Richard now stopped realising what he had said, it had happened again the past and the present had intertwined.

A voice now came from somewhere at the back of the hall. 'I was at Fountains yesterday but didn't see any stone bee hive, if it's the bit I think you are talking about there are only a load of stones at the bottom of a foundation wall'.

Piers now stood up thinking that Richard really had gone too far this time, what the hell was he talking about. He walked over and tapped Richard on the shoulder 'Think it best if you just sit down old man'. Richard looked at Piers and nodded his head gently.

He returned to his seat and was aware of Tom Maitland leaning over towards him.

'Is that the rest of the story we didn't hear last night' he said laughing. Piers turned round and glowered at Tom who took the hint and shut up.

Piers turned back to the audience and held his hands up 'I'm sure we would all like to say a big thank you now to Richard for what was such an interesting and informative talk which has also provided us with a lot of food for thought'. The murmuring in the audience now died down and a gentle clapping of hands followed. 'Without further ado I will hand you back to Professor Applewhite who will continue with today's proceedings, thank you'.

Piers turned round and motioned to Richard to go with him and as they left the hall many eyes followed Richard as he walked out of the conference door. 'Let's go to the bar we can have a quiet chat there, hopefully it won't be too busy' said Piers. Richard nodded and his mind started to race as he knew what was coming, how could he explain things and come up with something plausible. In the Coronation bar and after two steaming hot filter coffees had been delivered to their table Piers folded his hands together and looked at Richard.

'What's going on, is everything alright' Piers asked.

Richard cleared his throat and knew that he would have to give an Oscar performance. 'Yes I'm fine, really. You know me Piers I get so enthused about things and sometimes carried away'. On the way back from the conference hall he decided that one of his courses of action was just to sideline it all, immerse it and blind him with science. 'It's this black bee idea, I've been working on it for some time now and really see a lot of possibilities, we could do it, set up a comprehensive breeding programme and see what happens'.

'And what about this Adolphus fellow' said Piers still looking at him suspiciously.

'Oh him, just a figment of my imagination, why what else did you think it was' said Richard firmly putting the ball back in Piers court.

'I'm not sure, it's just that when you were talking it all sounded so convincing' said Piers.

'You know me, always could tell a good story, you believed it' said Richard now visibly starting to relax as he felt the pressure ease off of him'.

The moment had somehow passed and Piers motioned to the waitress to bring them two more coffees. 'I'm most interested in this breeding programme, with the black honeybee' said Piers.

'Yes I've been doing a bit of research and also spoken to BIBBA' said Richard. Piers sat forward and put this hands together.

'The Bee Improvement and Bee Breeders' Association' said Piers, 'I believe we have one or two of their people here at the conference'.

'So I understand, it's quite a challenge for us all I believe'.

'On Monday come and see me and we can have a proper talk' said Piers now draining his coffee cup. 'I must get back to the conference, take it easy Richard and by the way I'm not expecting to see you here any more'.

'Am I banned' said Richard looking at Piers.

'No but you work too hard Richard, take a break, take it easy and I'll see you next week'. He patted Richard on the shoulder as he passed him on his way out of the bar and Richard now felt somewhat at a lose end. He knew that another trip was inevitable but somehow felt uneasy about taking it from the hotel, it just didn't feel safe any more. It was then that the idea came to him that another visit to Fountains Abbey was the solution, he could take his trip there and be completely anonymous, away from it all and also he thought to himself very appropriately the scene of the crime.

CHAPTER FOURTEEN

Richard jumped into his car and slammed it in first gear, the open road ahead of him. He followed the same route as the day before through the village of Marton-le-Moor and then on to the B6265 to Fountains Abbey. His previous trip had been on a typical Spring day with a pale blue rinsed sky and a gentle breeze but today it was grey and overcast with a definite threat of rain.

As he drew into the half empty car park Richard concluded that the inclement weather had probably put a lot of people off and this he thought would be to his advantage. He would find a quiet secluded part of the abbey, a spot with a good vantage point and then the sting. At the ticket office he handed over his money and pocketed the slip that gained him entrance to the abbey grounds. In the enclosure he spotted the uniformed figure of the National Trust guide though this time it wasn't Adam but an older man who shepherded the small group that was now with him.

He knew that over the other side of the Great Court lay the fine remains of the *reredorter* and adjoining it the lay brothers infirmary. Though most of this building had long since gone it still had some fairly high walls and it was to one of these that Richard now made his way. He found a grassy bank on a south facing wall and removed the rucksack from his back. Carefully releasing the catches he took a small container out and placed it on the ground in front of him and even with the lid closed he could hear the gentle buzz of the bee inside. He looked down the valley and now saw the first of the rain that threatened earlier start to descend and thought how different it felt to the last time he was here, a typical Spring day but no longer. The light shower had now become quite a downpour and he watched as a number of figures further down the valley make a run for it. He had brought a waterproof with him that he now extracted from his rucksack and pulled over his head rolling the right hand sleeve up to his elbow. Picking the small container up he opened the lid carefully and with his tweezers grasped the bee inside. It was that moment again of instant pain and then the wait. As he watched the figures in their brightly coloured waterproofs run for cover they suddenly disappeared and the first thing he noticed was that the rain had stopped and the sun was shining, he had gone back.

Hearing the sound of voices he turned round and watched Adolphus and Conan approach him heavily engrossed in conversation. He strained his ears to listen but as they passed him their conversation stopped, not on his account of course as he was totally invisible to them. He gathered his rucksack and followed them down past the River Skell and out into the open valley area, they walked at a fast pace and he broke into a gentle trot behind them. Richard noticed how different everything looked, there was a different skyline with shorter trees, less foliage, a younger earth, a time when the Domesday Book had only been written a hundred years ago. They now came to a small wooden bridge that crossed the River Skell and they halted temporarily to look over the side at the fast running river below where the reeds danced beneath the surface in the strong current.

'William Jerome is at the grange now' said Conan 'He told me yesterday that he was going to the mill to check the grinding of the oats and barley but I sense there may be another reason'.

'And that is' said Adolphus.

'The trout in Malham Tarn and a secret meeting with William de Percy our benefactor who granted us these fishing rights some twenty years ago'. Adolphus waited for Conan to continue. 'I have had word from the Kitchener that our fish is in short supply for some reason though I have no idea why as the monks tell me how plentiful their catch has been, I am the grange master and responsible'.

Adolphus stroked his jaw and turned to Conan 'You are a good grange master my friend and want to protect yourself, I too would be the same with my bees and that reminds me we must check the skeps before we return to the abbey today' Conan nodded silently in agreement.

The pair now turned and continued over the bridge and Richard dutifully followed close behind them. After about some twenty minutes they left the soft valley floor and he saw up ahead a large grey two storey building with small slit like openings that sat on the far side of a large lake and Richard thought to himself that this must be the corn mill on Malham Tarn that they had spoken about. As they neared the mill he could see the huge wheel turning effortlessly and the light green weeds of the lake tenaciously hanging onto the spokes as it rotated and submerged over and over again. Adolphus and Conan now stopped and looked up and down the lake until Conan pointed towards the mill. Richard too had spotted a figure that had appeared from around the corner of the mill and quickly disappeared into the undergrowth obviously not wishing to be seen. He hurried to catch up with the others and just caught the end of their conversation.

'Did you see him' said Conan 'William Jerome my suspicions were right, he was about no good that's for sure'.

They peered to see where he had gone but he was soon lost in the deep foliage further round the lake side. They stood and watched for a few minutes and then made their way towards the mill and as he followed the others in their footsteps all that could be heard was the thunderous roar of the wheel that had become louder and louder. Now almost alongside he watched as the rainbow spray of the water lifted into the warm sunlit afternoon and floated off in the air across the lake. Richard became lost in the moment and pulled himself together remembering the last time this had happened in the cellarium and he was locked in the store room. He turned around and the others had already disappeared and he swore quietly to himself under his breath.

A few steps took him around the back of the mill building and he spotted a small arched doorway on the far side. As he entered it took a few moments for his eyes to adjust to the darkness and also now what was the deafening noise of the heavy grinding equipment. In the middle of the floor a pair of grindstones turned quickly making a low rumbling sound and two of the brothers stood close by sweeping the immediate area as clouds of dust from the grain rose up to the ceiling. A ladder in the corner led to the upper floor and Richard now climbed the steep rungs carefully clinging onto the rails as a long drop lay beneath him. He pulled himself up at the top and saw as he looked around that this was the grain store. The air was thick and dry and he coughed copiously fearing that this lungs would explode, how did the monks manage he wondered. At the far end of the floor he spotted Adolphus and Conan who were busy with some sacking in the corner and he watched as Conan lifted two large fish into the air waiving them around, his suspicions were right.

'Jerome has an accomplice, one of the monks no doubt, whoever he is the priest will have much to hear in his confession' said Conan.

Adolphus nodded 'Who do you think it is'

'Brother Thomas, I have often wondered about his commitment to the order and a shifty character as well'.

'What now'.

'Jerome is long gone to collect his rewards from de Percy, there is nothing more that can be done here, we must speak to the Abbot. Come we will visit your skeps and then back to the abbey'.

The pair passed by Richard almost brushing him as they reached the ladder to descend below. Richard followed them and waited as they stopped to speak to one of the brothers and then left by the small arched doorway. They did not return to the front of the mill but made their way down a small track that led further away from the valley area and Richard looking at the sun deduced that the grange must lay south of the abbey enclosure.

A ten minute walk took them to a large impressive manor house surrounded by tall strong trees that now swung in the afternoon breeze. The granges were demesne farms first developed by the Cistercians in the 12th century and converted from tenanted manors that were not only home to the lay brothers but also a source of hospitality for any passers by. Richard concluded that in our own way we were all passers by in this life until we shuffled off this mortal coil, here but for a brief second in time, here to do our best and hopefully leave it a better place than when we arrived. He wondered what his legacy would be, the bees of course he smiled to himself. He couldn't wait to see Adolphus' skeps and made his way around the side of the grange to a large garden at the rear. He recognised a number of lay brothers by their short tunics and loose hair busy hoeing a vegetable patch with their crude tools, the sweat running freely down their faces in the warm afternoon sun. Some distance away down a slope he spotted Conan and Adolphus standing by what must be the skeps and a closer inspection by Richard showed them to be wicker baskets plastered with mud and dung. Adolphus had pulled over his head a strange looking contraption that looked like a cage with a cloth over the front of his face. His hands were left bare, brave man Richard thought to himself as he pulled the top off the skep and proceeded to remove the honey, the bees buzzing angrily around him.

'They have been busy, very busy, see the honey here a plentiful supply to eat and also of course to make candles'. He stood up and looked around him 'Mathias, where are you'. A short man appeared who proceeded to help Adolphus remove the honey from the skep, his hands busy and quick, obviously more than used to the task.

'We must get back to the abbey' said Conan and Adolphus nodded in agreement. They made their way to the front of the grange and down the track towards the mill house and some thirty minutes later arrived at the abbey. Richard was puffing and quite out of breath, he was impressed with the stamina of these monks, so hardy and strong by comparison to us modern day weaklings he thought.

'Abbot Deyer will be in the chapter house for prayers now, we can slip in and speak to him afterwards' said Conan. But they never made it to the chapter house because as they walked across the cloister green there was an horrendous noise, the loudest rumbling you could imagine and the green rippled like the sea in front of them, it was an earthquake. Richard never saw what happened to the others as he stumbled and felt a sharp pain on his cheek and looking down saw that he had tripped over the grassy bank and cut his face on some stones. He got to his knees and looking around him saw nothing now but the ruins of the abbey and some people rushing over to him with a very concerned look on their faces asking him if he was alright and because of the terrible state he was in should they call for some medical assistance, he had gone back.

CHAPTER FIFTEEN

He was helped by a group of people back to the cafeteria where they waited for a first aider to arrive. A cup of strong tea with four sugars was put in front of him that he was ordered to drink. He held a large piece of cotton wool to his cheek that was still bleeding profusely and hurt like hell. One of the ladies hovering said 'We just don't know what happened, one minute you were standing there and then you walked straight into the bank almost as if it wasn't there' she said. Although she didn't know it of course she was exactly right as the bank had not been there when Richard walked across the flat cloister green.

'I wasn't looking where I was going, that's all' mumbled Richard now becoming rather tired of the undue attention he was now attracting.

'Where is the patient' a voice called out and a young rather attractive woman now pushed her way through the crowd to the table. The group moved back and she bent to examine Richard's face. 'I'm Eleanor and that's a rather nasty cut, it might need some stitches'.

'I'm sure it will be o.k. once the bleeding has stopped' he said pressing the cold compress she had now applied to his cheek. Richard looked at her as she tended to him and thought what a beautiful looking creature she was with long golden hair and eyes of the deepest blue, truly his angel of mercy.

'We'll see how we get on with this bleeding, it does look rather a deep cut' said Eleanor'. Richard suddenly remembered Conan and Adolphus and wondered if they too had been injured in the earthquake and needed something stitching up. He shuddered to think of the basic treatment they would have received and thought how glad he was that he had made it back to the present time. He released the compress from his face and looked at Eleanor.

'How is it looking' he asked.

She bent her face near to the wound and told him that although the bleeding had stopped it still looked bad.

'Have you a mirror, let me see what it looks like' said Richard. Eleanor fumbled in her medical bag and produced a small mirror that he now peered into, he shrugged his shoulders, 'it should soon heal up'.

'I think you'll have a scar though, but probably not if you get it stitched' she said.

'No I'm fine, really'.

Eleanor fumbled in her bag once again and produced a book 'I have to record the accident and also that you refused hospital treatment' she said. She clicked a ball point pen and started to write asking Richard for details every so often. When she had finished she turned the book around and gave Richard the pen asking him to sign the entry.

'Did you drive here today' she asked putting the book back in her bag. Richard nodded that he had and was told that he ought to wait for an hour or so before getting behind the wheel, just in case he started feeling woozy. No sooner had she arrived than she was gone and Richard now sat in an empty café looking out of the window. He decided that he would have to tell Susan that he was at Fountains Abbey and fell on some masonry, simple as that. He also decided that he was not going to face any of the others back at the Mitre Hotel and any more of their questions. He would string his time out here, return later when he knew they would be at dinner, pack his bag check out and with a bit of luck be home around midnight when Susan would already be in bed. It would give his face a chance to maybe heal a little and not look quite so bad in the morning.

'Would you like another cup of tea' a voice asked from the serving counter.

Richard turned round and said that he would and also was a cheese roll possible. She was a middle aged woman with a kindly face and grey wispy hair who told him not to worry and she would see he was alright. He thanked her and turned back to his private thoughts. Tomorrow he would go to the library and see his Professor, what was his name Clive, that was it Clive Durnley and have a chat with him, the quantum mechanics man. Another thing he needed to check out was this earthquake, if it had been recorded he would know the exact date that he had been there. Another cup of tea and a crusty roll were put in front of him by the kindly waitress who told him not to worry and take as long as he wanted. 'Are there many accidents here at the Abbey with people and the masonry' asked Richard taking a large bite out of his roll.

'Oh yes, even with those signs up all over the place and especially kids'.

'So it's not just me' said Richard joking.

'No, and you won't be the last that's for sure' she said.

After Richard had finished eating and drained his tea cup he stood up and steadied himself for a few seconds, the first aider had been right and he did feel a bit woozy. He just needed to take it slowly and not rush. 'Well thank you for looking after me, how much do I owe you' he said walking over to the counter.

'Nothing sir, you just take it easy now' she replied.

Richard smiled and made his way out of the café and across the outer court to the car park. There was only one other car left there apart from his own as most of the people had departed early on account of the bad weather. Slipping behind the wheel he turned the ignition key and the engine sprang into life, he couldn't wait to get back to the hotel and more importantly back to Susan, he had missed her.

He took a slow drive and wished in some ways he could just climb into bed back at the hotel but didn't want to risk being around and, more importantly being seen with his cut face, yet more questions he thought to himself. At the hotel reception when he collected his room key a note was handed to him by the receptionist that had been left in his pigeon hole, it was from Piers saying that he wanted to have a drink with him later on in the bar. He screwed the message up and poked it into his pocket, no way thought Richard making a quick exit to his room at the back of the hotel. It took no more than minutes to empty his wardrobe and gather his wash things together before he was back at the reception desk to settle his bill. He scribbled a note for Piers telling him that he was needed back home and would see him on Monday.

'We hope you enjoyed your stay with us Mr Fellowes, was everything alright' the receptionist enquired.

'Yes, just fine thank you, goodbye'.

It had only taken about two hours to drive down and Richard guessed that going back would be something in the region of about three hours on account of the fact that he would take it easy. He checked his face in the car mirror and thought that he would get a plaster on it back home, that way it would hide the worst of it. The roads were kind as it was the midweek lull and at 10 o'clock he pulled up at the front of No. 27 Hereford Row. Looking up he saw the bedroom was in darkness and knew that Susan had already turned in. He felt exhausted as he lifted his suitcase out of the boot and made his way to the front door, a quick visit to the bedroom to kiss Susan goodnight and then a very large Jack Daniels he decided. Upstairs he pushed the bedroom door open and quietly crept to the bedside 'It's me darling' he said bending to plant a kiss on her cheek.

'Glad to hear it otherwise I would think I was about to be ravaged by some stranger' she murmured. She reached out to turn the bedside light on and Richard quickly caught her hand before she got to the switch.

'Don't disturb yourself, go back to sleep' he said.

'I thought that you were staying until tomorrow'.

'I was but there was no need, I did everything I had to' he replied. 'I won't be long, just going to have a quick drink and I'll be up'.

'Ok' she murmured drifting off back to sleep.

Downstairs Richard opened the drinks cupboard and poured a Jack Daniels that he swilled back in one go. Just one more and then to bed. He then rememberd the present he had bought for Susan and retrieved it from his bag, he would put it on her bedside table and she could open it first thing in the morning. He remembered that he should put a plaster on his cheek and made a visit to the bathroom before going to bed. Turning the light on he looked in the mirror and was somewhat taken aback at the state of his face, the first aider had been right it needed stitching. At the back of the cupboard were some butterfly strips and he carefully strapped them across the wound to bind the skin together as much as he could before finally putting a plaster over the whole area. He would see how it was tomorrow and if necessary go to the hospital and get it sorted out. Yes the hospital first and then the library, or maybe just the library, he would see.

He put his pjamas on and slipped into bed next to Susan. What a few days, so much had happened, it was only Monday that he had gone to Fountains but it felt like weeks ago. He winced as he felt a pain shoot across his face and spared a thought for the monks, he wondered what injuries they had sustained and imagined that it had probably turned into something of a very busy night at the Monks Infirmary in Fountains Abbey.

CHAPTER SIXTEEN

'Richard it's beautiful' said Susan as she unwrapped her present.

'I have been reliably informed that it is Edwardian and knew that you would love it' he said.

'I do but you are very naughty, it must have cost a fair bit'.

'It did but your worth it' he replied planting a kiss on her cheek. She turned to look at him and gasped, 'What's happened to your face Richard'.

'Oh just a silly fall when I was at Fountains, on some stones, it's really unsafe some of it. I'll keep an eye on it, don't worry'. he replied.

'Are you going to the office today'.

'No I'm back tomorrow. I need to go to the library, do you fancy meeting for lunch in town'.

'Yes that would be nice, there's a new bar that has opened up and from all accounts is very good, 'Hugo's' on the main square'.

'Fine with me, I'll see you there at 1 o'clock.

'I could come to the library with you'.

'No really don't bother, I'll see you later'. Richard wanted to talk with the Professor and wasn't keen on Susan being privy to their conversation.

'As you want, I must shower and get going'. She leant across the bed and kissed Richard thanking him again for her present and he winced. 'Keep an eye on that cut, do you think it might be better to leave it uncovered, let the air get to it'.

'Yes, but not yet, it needs to bind together a bit first of all' he said.

Susan left about 11 o'clock and Richard closely followed her, she to the shops and he to the library. As he entered its elegant portal he hoped that the Professor would be there and not his day off or something. Through the archway of the history section he was delighted to see Clive Durnley sitting behind his small desk in the corner. He looked up as Richard walked over to him and he gave a broad smile.

'I wondered if I might see you again and it looks like you have been in the wars' the Professor said pointing to Richard's face.

'Oh yes, it happened at Fountains Abbey actually, wasn't looking where I was going and the next thing I knew I was on the ground with a very sore face'.

The professor nodded and asked if there was anything in particular that he needed help with.

'Well I was wondering if I could have a chat with you actually, it's this quantum mechanics thing'.

'Well that's a very big area your talking about' said the Professor 'Is there any particular angle'.

Richard took a moment before he replied 'Do you think that it's possible to travel back in time'. The professor raised his eyebrows and let out a small breath.

'What an interesting question, well humans are in fact always travelling in time, in a linear fashion from the present to the immediate future, inexorably until death. The common belief held is that it would be more viable to travel forward in time, but you want to go back'. Richard nodded his head and waited for him to continue. 'If wormholes could be created it might be possible to construct closed time like loops in space-time which may allow for the possibility of time travel. In quantum mechanics we talk about the multiverse, many universes co-existing so it gets you out of trouble by allowing time to evolve differently if you succeed in going back to a previous time'. The expression on Richard's face told the professor that he was having difficulty in absorbing what he had said. 'No it's not easy is it, shall I carry on'. Richard nodded again and the professor continued. 'Another school of thought is FTL, the faster than light hypothesis. Basically the closer you come to the speed of light the slower time will go, but lets take a short break I'm due a cup of coffee about this time, come and join me'.

They made their way to the floor above into the café and Richard waited while the professor joined the queue. Richard thought that so far he had heard nothing to explain his predicament and how this bee venom had allowed him to travel back in time. He toyed with the idea of letting the professor in on his secret but knew deep down that Susan should have been his confidante in all this, he could already see her face with a horrified expression and a promise extracted from him that he would never ever do it again, a promise he would not, could not give. Two cups of steaming hot coffee were now placed on the table and the gentle wise old eyes of the professor looked at him.

'While I was in the queue it came to me that I don't know your name' he said.

'No I'm sorry, it's Richard Fellowes'.

'And when you came in the other day Richard I seem to recall your particular interest in the 12th century and the monks at Fountains Abbey, it's not in any way connected with your question today about time travel' he said half jokingly. Richard fidgeted in his seat feeling rather uneasy about the way the conversation was heading, in some way it would have made more sense if he could of told him what had happened but not here, not now.

'No it's just something that has always interested me and when you told me the other day you were a Phd Quantum Mechanics, well I knew you were the person I should talk with'.

'Ok, well the next thing we need to consider in relation to time travel is entropy, the thermodynamic arrow of time that results from the fact that there are always many more disordered states than ordered ones. A classic example of this is the jigsaw puzzle in a box, there is only one arrangement that makes a complete picture but in comparison a huge number of arrangements that are disordered and can never make a picture. Time can only move forward in one direction'. He stopped and looked at Richard 'I hope that what I have told you makes some sense and attempts to answer your question'.

'Do you believe Professor we could go back in time, despite everything you have said'.

The professor carefully returned his cup to its saucer and looked up. 'I always think of the famous grandfather paradox and the obvious answer it seems to give. If you could go back and kill your grandfather before your father was born, et cetera, et cetera, you understand'.

Richard sat quietly, the lecture was now over. 'Thank you professor for your time, and that wasn't meant to be a joke by the way'.

'You are welcome, if you want to talk any more you know where I am'.

Richard leant forward and shook his hand 'Goodbye for now'.

CHAPTER SEVENTEEN

As Richard made his way back down the stairs he mulled over in his mind the possibility of taking the professor into his confidence, it was something that he needed to think about very carefully and all the possible implications involved. He was sure that his first reaction would be disbelief which of course would naturally lead to a trip, a trip with the professor, what a prospect he savoured.

He remembered that he was going to check up on that date for the earthquake but totally forgot about it after his discussion with the professor on time travel, never mind he thought that was something he could do later on at home. He met for lunch as arranged with Susan at Hugo's, an establishment that Richard decided was over rated as well as over priced and spent an otherwise uneventful day.

Friday dawned a bright sunny day and a complete turnaround with the weather that had been so changeable. Richard had decided late in bed last night that Friday offered a perfect opportunity to trip as Susan would be out at the charity shop all day. At 7 o'clock he opened his eyes and gave a low moan and turned over in bed. 'What's wrong Richard is your face troubling you' she said.

'No I've got terrible toothache, it's been giving me hell all night' Richard replied.

'Well I'm not surprised as you never keep your appointment for check-ups' she said.

'I'll give them a ring when the surgery opens and see what happens'. A quick call to the office later and he would tell them an emergency route canal was needed and his day would be free.

Some two hours later Susan closed the front door and Richard quickly dressed and opened his lap top. He tapped in earthquakes in England during the 12th century and sat staring at the screen which in due course reliably informed him that the exact date he had gone back to was Wednesday 15th April 1185 when a large earthquake threw down houses and badly damaged Lincoln cathedral. The quake was described in the old medieval annais as having been felt throughout England although the precise location of the epicentre was obscure. It was thought that the earthquake must have been around five or even larger in magnitude and he wondered how badly the monks had been affected and hoped their casuality list was not too large. Another factor of course concerning the earthquake was the indisputable proof it provided that he had really gone back in time, first he had the initials carved on the column in the *cellarium* and now this.

Richard remembered that he needed to ring the office and give his excuses for the day and wondered how much news had got back concerning his speech at the seminar. It was a rather unfortunate incident to say the least but felt he had done well in allaying the fears that Piers initially expressed by his talk of a breeding programme with the black honeybee. The phone rang for just a few seconds until Brian Dawes' secretary promptly answered his call and

Richard explained to her that he would be on a day's sick leave due to emergency dental work and he would see them all on Monday. He replaced the phone in its cradle and scratched his head, the time had come for his next trip. He checked that all the doors were secure and made his way to the small laboratory at the back of the house. He carefully closed the door behind him and in one step was the other side of the room and reached for the small box on the shelf where the last of the bees had been deposited. Over the past few days he had managed three trips and this one now would see the last of his *apis melaffera*.

With what had now turned into an almost casual routine procedure Richard pulled up his sleeve and jabbed the bee into his arm, again the second of agony that was quickly replaced by a dull throb. He wasn't sure how long it took but felt the transition on this occasion had been a fairly quick one as he no longer saw the wall in front of him but a long line of young ash trees, he was on a dusty track and to his left lay the nave of the abbey church. He sensed the weather was far warmer with a burning sun and a deep blue sky, the blooms of the unmistakeable rhododendrums, azaleas and oleanders told him that it was mid summer now and some eight weeks had surely passed since his last trip when it had been Easter time. Richard then remembered the earthquake and looking over towards the abbey saw that nothing appeared different, all the buildings were there as before and had evidently escaped any damage.

Some movement up ahead of Richard attracted his attention. He looked down towards the gatehouse and outer court area to see a colourful pageantry of flags and banners with horse drawn carriages that were making their way to the front of the abbey. Richard quickly walked nearer to the gatehouse and the approaching entourage, on the front carriage fluttered a red and gold flag, the royal colours of the monarchy and it would seem a visit by none other than King Henry II. Richard thought about the many conversations he had been privy to about the empty coffers and, in particular, the exchange that he had heard that day in the abbot's quarters between the abbot and the bishop about the huge expenses incurred by the Royal court. He wondered what had precipitated this visit now and concluded that matters had moved on since his last visit some two months ago.

Richard had done his homework and knew the abbey came under the jurisdiction of Bishop Hugh Chaloner and therefore the King himself. May be the explanation given for the obedentaries by Jerome, Heribert and Gower had failed to satisfy after all and furthermore what of Jerome and the missing trout. Of course he did not know the outcome of Adolphus and Conan's visit to the abbot that afternoon as the earthquake had intervened and he vehemently hoped they had survived, so many unanswered questions he thought to himself.

The sound of lilting music now drifted across the warm balmy air, a flute and a gentle stringed instrument played by some finely dressed courtiers in a carriage to the rear of the procession. He now saw at close hand the King who looked a strongly built muscular character with a freckled face and red hair cut very short. Richard knew that he would be King for just another four years, but his reign had been tainted since his involvement with the death of Thomas Beckett in 1170 when four of his knights, Reginald Fitzurse, Hugh de Morville, William de Tracy and Richard le Breton had gone to Canterbury Cathedral and cut him down, something he had later very much come to regret. It seemed none were somehow spared his infamous temper when in 1173 he placed his wife Eleanor of Aquitaine under house arrest after she had encouraged their children to rebel against him.

A huge group of monks now surged out the front of the abbey into the Great Court and it was with huge relief that Richard spotted Adolphus and Conan near the front of the crowd, his friends had been spared the earthquake. The music stopped and the King now stepped down aided by three of his nobles and Richard was able to see the strong curved legs and horseman's shins so aptly described in the historical description he had read about him. The abbot in his finest liturgical vestments stepped forward and knelt to kiss the outstretched hand of the King.

'Your majesty, welcome to Fountains Abbey, it is our great pleasure to receive you and your court' said the Abbot as he rose to his feet. Richard wondered how much of that was true and hurt him to have to utter those words as surely the opposite must have been the case.

'My abbot we are pleased that you receive us hot and tired as we may be, our journey from London has taken some twenty days. The journey has been slow with many stops, at Nottingham castle not a week gone by and some three days ago our court was at Barnard castle'. But one castle that Richard was sure he would not have visited was Northampton, the scene of the trial for poor Thomas Beckett. 'I trust all is ready for us' said the King. Again Richard thought of the empty coffers and wondered what delicacies the kitchener would be able to provide for the hungry bellies of this huge entourage.

'Yes sire, all is in place. Our Bishop Chaloner will be with us on the morrow'.

The King nodded his head 'Then we shall have much to talk about'.

Richard looked at the abbot and saw his brow was furrowed and detected a resigned expression. Something was afoot and it seemed that all was not well.

The abbot turned and raised his arm pointing to the East and West guest houses 'Sire your quarters are well appointed, the East guest house has a fine balcony with views over the river'. The king nodded his head and turned to his courtier who stood by his side.

'Make haste and make ready' he instructed his loyal servant. The entourage now slowly moved across the Great Court, the King cutting a fine figure as he strode boldly to the East guest house with the remainder of the party following on foot and the carriages trundling behind. A great flurry of activity then ensued with large trunks being transferred to the guest houses and courtiers running to and fro with the possessions of their masters. Richard looked around and spotted Adolphus and Conan loitering by a doorway leading to the cellarium. He walked towards them and saw they were in heavy conversation but could not hear them as he was still out of earshot. He quickened his pace to join them as he heard Adolphus say.

'There is much talk of Henry Cuylter, the sacrist at York being a possible successor to Linus Deyer who it is said will not see another Michelmas as our abbot'.

'Yes I too have heard the same, Cuylter's talents have not gone unnoticed and he has a safe pair of hands too. None of the gold or silver at York has ever gone missing while in his care' replied Conan.

'Abbot Deyer has been a great spiritual leader for us but may be now is the time for a man with more of a grasp on temporal matters.

Conan eyed Adolphus and at length uttered 'Timothy 6 verses 10-12, money is the root of all evil but we are nothing without it' he said with a resigned expression on his face.

'Yes but used wisely and honestly it can bring many good things by the grace of God and we must pray for those amongst us who have been tempted by the devil and given way it seems' replied Adolphus.

'Then remember William Jerome tonight as you kneel obediently by your bed' said Conan. So he had abused his position as Cellarer and the fishing rights at Malham Tarn as he recalled that day he had been spotted acting suspiciously and heading off for a clandestine meeting with William de Percy. But the earthquake had not thwarted their quest to speak with Abbot Deyer it would seem and obviously events had unfolded with Richard assumed the dismissal of Jerome, heads had started to roll and this must be part of the reason for the King's visit and a transition of power it now seemed. The Bishop would be with them the next day and Richard agonised over the fact that it was highly unlikely he would be privy to that meeting as his time would have run out and, when he returned on his next trip, events would have moved on.

Adolphus and Conan now turned and went through the entrance into the cellarium but Richard did not follow them. He looked back towards the guest houses and made his way through the Great Court that was now quiet and empty after the flurry of activity earlier and watched as the last of the horses were released from their shafts and led away to the stables. He walked through the yard over to the outer window of the east guest house and peered through to see the King now reposed in a chair and being fussed by his courtiers in attendance. It was a large room and quite resplendent with fine furnishings and on the table Richard noticed what must have been the finest silverware released by the sacrist for this special occasion, beautiful goblets and shiny tureens, he wondered if that sacrist had been Henry Gower or another with its temporary care. The king now stood up and walked over towards the window and peered through looking straight at him, Richard caught his breath and stood back wondering if at last he had become visible in that other world. The king was now waiving at him and as he looked closer saw that it was in fact no longer the king but Susan with a very puzzled expression on her face, he had gone back.

Chapter Eighteen

The warm mid summer afternoon had now gone and it was pouring with rain. Richard quickly pulled himself together and turned to see Susan walking round the corner from the back of the house.

'Richard what on earth are you doing standing out here in this weather looking through the window and from the look on your face it seemed you thought I was someone else'.

Oh God Richard thought another load of explanations. 'Well you keep reminding me that I've got a lot of jobs to do still and I was just checking the woodwork on this window to see if we need to replace it'.

'What in this weather Richard, are you mad and what about the dentist, did you go?'.

Another lie coming up he thought as he said 'Yes and I've got an appointment next week, as it happens the pain has eased off a lot and with a few paracetemol should keep things at bay till it gets treated'. A silence hung in the air between them as Susan looked at him.

'Come on let's go indoors and get you dried down, your hair is soaking wet'. He followed behind her like a naughty child and once they were in the kitchen she threw a towel over to him and reached for the kettle. 'A hot cup of tea is what you need to warm you up, you look quite pale'.

Richard gave a final wipe to his hair and made for the doorway 'I think I need something a bit stronger than that, a glass of whisky'.

'And that's another thing Richard, you seem to be drinking rather a lot these days and I'm sure it can't be good for you' she said.

'Medicinal purposes love, also it will help with my tooth'. In the sitting room he breathed a quiet sigh of relief as he opened the drinks cupboard and poured a large Jack Daniels and wondered if she believed his story. The telephone rang in the hall and he thought to himself saved by the bell.

'Richard can you get that' Susan called out to him.

'Yes no problem' he replied. In the hallway he lifted the handset to hear Frances her sister at the other end of the line and after the usual meaningless exchanges was told that she needed to speak with her sister quite urgently.

'It's Frances for you, said its urgent' Richard called out to Susan as he beat a hasty retreat back to the drinks cupboard to refill his glass and then hover by the door to hear about what was so urgent.

'Yes I quite understand your predicament and I can't see any reason why there should be a problem'. There was a silence as Frances continued the conversation at the other end of the line and after a few moments Susan replied 'No I'll give Vanessa a call now and then give you a call back to confirm everything, don't worry it will be o.k.'. The hall went silent and Susan came to find Richard who was now sitting leafing through a magazine the far side of the room.

'Everything o.k. love' he said glancing up at her.

'Frances is in a right state, in short she's run out of time off of work and she needs me to go over and look after Joshua for a fortnight, would that be alright with you'.

Richard could hardly contain his glee and struggled to keep a straight expression on his face. 'No you must go and help out, I'll be fine here and perhaps it might be best all round if Robyn could go and stay with friends, you know I'm in and out all the time'.

'There wasn't a problem before about this time off thing but her boss is away and his deputy is something of a bastard, so there we are. I just need to check with Vanessa about my Friday slot at work and then I'll sort the rest out from there'. She checked her watch and told him that now was a good time to catch her and disappeared into the hall. He listened to her dial the number and sat back in his chair with his hands behind his head, what a gift this was as he savoured the thought of two unbridled weeks ahead of him and the opportunities that afforded. Free time, free space and he now decided in his euphoric state that he would tell the Professor everything, he would take him into his confidence. He couldn't help smiling to himself and had to quickly pull himself together as Susan came in.

'I've spoken to Vanessa and everything is o.k., I'm leaving on Sunday but we can sort things out here over the weekend before I go'.

Richard nodded his head and told her not to worry about anything as he was going to be extra busy with this black bee breeding programme and quite a few trips to the BIBBA headquarters over the next few weeks. She wasn't listening though as already in her head she was going through the arrangements and no doubt starting her what to do list. A final telephone call to her sister completed the exercise after which Susan informed him that she was off for a long soak in the bath and would he be good enough to collect the ritual Friday night curry.

A short drive delivered Richard to the door of the Little Delhi restaurant some three streets away and he was pleased to see that it was early enough to miss the Friday night throng of customers.

'Good evening sir, and what is your pleasure tonight' said Mr Kurapati to Richard as he walked into what could be described as a mini India with the strumming of the sitars in his ears and the mass of foliage to the extent that he felt somewhat like Dr. Livingstone.

'I just need your takeaway service' said Richard reaching for a menu off the counter. He decided that tonight was a bit of a celebration really what with Susan off to her sister and also as far as he was concerned the wonderful freedom that lay ahead of him. He eyed the menu in front of him and said 'Well to start we will have two onion bhajis, followed by Lamb Pasanda with Kashmiri rice and to round it off a portion of Aloo Gobi'.

'A very good choice sir' said Mr Kurapati to Richard as he finished writing the order and passed it through a hatch behind him.

'My wife usually collects our order' said Richard 'Mrs Fellowes I'm sure you know her'.

'Yes a delightful lady' said Mr Kurapati' but tonight it is you'.

'Yes, she is very busy as a sudden family crisis has called her away. Her sister's boy has a badly broken leg and she needs to be there for her family' Richard replied.

'Oh I know all about broken legs, my youngest Ganesh is always breaking or bruising something' Mr Kurapati replied 'many a night we have sat in the casualty department waiting for an x-ray'.

Richard looked at Mr Kurapati's coffee coloured face and decided that he was a man who possessed strong features with a long straight nose, wide full lips and eyes that were deep brown, so brown that they almost looked like pools of liquid chocolate. He wasn't tall but medium in height with a compact body and biceps that bulged under his tee shirt, did he work out at the gym Richard wondered, did Indians in general work out or maybe they worked out anyway as they jostled their way through their busy cities going about their daily business. Richard heard the tail end of a sentence as Mr Kurapati informed him that they were going to be closed in October as they were going back home to celebrate Diwali, the festival of lights with the rest of his family.

The hatch opened and a large brown carrier bag was deposited on the shelf behind Mr Kurapati that he swiftly placed on the counter in front of Richard with a slip of paper informing him that he owed £20.50 for the meal. As he handed over a £20 note and a 50 pence coin that Richard informed him was the exact money, he noticed Mr Kurapati had a very nasty swelling on the side of his hand. He saw Richard staring at it and gave a small laugh 'Oh that it's nothing serious just a bee sting I got the other day. It happened here would you believe it but I was so lucky with such a large supply of onions in my kitchen at the back that I quickly rubbed in to help the pain'. Richard looked up at him and asked.

'And have you had any other ill effects'.

'No nothing, I am not allergic to bee stings so I'm fine'.

Richard nodded thinking to himself that surely it must be the venom from the bees with the Kashmiri virus that was the problem and healthy bees posed no threat. He had been stung in the past but never experienced this time change before, he would have to look more closely at the chemical make up of this Kashmiri virus to see if he could make any sense out of it as unlikely as that might be.

'Are you wanting a receipt' said Mr Kurapati to which Richard shook his head in reply as he made his way out of the takeaway and back to his car where he deposited the large brown carrier bag on the floor in front of the passenger seat. He noticed that a large greasy stain was already starting to spread down the side of the bag and wondered how much saturated fat there was in this meal, perhaps they should eat Chinese he thought it must be more healthy.

Back at Carrow Mansions Susan was sitting at the table checking her diary for any cancellations she might need to make and looked with surprise at the huge bag Richard put on the table in front of her. 'I didn't know we were expecting guests, there's enough here to feed an army'.

'Thought we would splash out a bit tonight, make a bit of a change you know' he said.

As Susan removed the foil lids from the containers and placed some spoons deep into their contents she told Richard that he must make sure Robyn came round for dinner while she was away.

'Yes but make sure that she rings me first of all, just to make sure I am here' said Richard as he thought to himself and not somewhere in the 12th century as he now took a large bite out of the onion bhaji that was perched precariously on the end of his fork.

CHAPTER NINETEEN

Piers Marchmont pushed his glasses down onto the bridge of his nose and stared intently at Richard the other side of the desk. 'So Richard what have you got for me'.

It was Monday morning and he was sitting in Pier's office at a meeting he had been ordered to last week after the debacle at conference to which luckily no further reference had been made.

'I have already spoken to Bob Jenkins at BIBBA and believe we can work together' said Richard.

'Yes and what does that involve' replied Piers.

'Well archaeological, biological and historical evidence show that honey bees in the UK from around 4,000 years ago up until the 19th century were genetically the dark European honey bee—*Apis mellifera mellifera*. Then from around 1814 a small number of Italian bee imports took place, mainly for experimental reasons. This continued until the early 1900's and then between 1916 and 1925 the British black bee was rendered almost extinct in England and Wales mainly due to acarine mite, better known as the 'Isle of Wight' disease. Pier's telephone rang and he put his hand up to temporarily halt their conversation.

'Yes I am aware of that but I'm in a meeting at the moment so call me back say in about an hour'. He replaced the receiver and looked attentively at Richard. 'Please continue'.

'Where was I, yes and after this 'Isle of Wight' disease there were major imports of Dutch and Italian bees and so it has continued with the addition of imports from the USA, Australia and New Zealand. One of the side effects of this is that the genetic mix of our honey bees has become very broad and although natural selection still favours dark bees, many of the major genetic advantages of the original native bee has been lost. Miles Glossop our technical man believes that it is this cross breeding with the Italian honeybee that has made the normally docile black bee very aggressive. Miles concurs with BIBBA over the possibility of re-introducing the black honeybee and, it is widely held, that there are wild populations throughout England from Scotland down to the West Country. Richard paused for a few moments and then continued. 'Scientists believe the insect that made honey for the tables of medieval kings could reverse the collapse of bee numbers that so far has endangered the annual pollination of crops worth around £165m.'

'And where does that leave us precisely Richard' said Piers leaning back in his chair and scratching the side of his face.

'I'm totally aware of my research work on this KBV but is it possible Piers that I could assist them with mapping these wild populations, obviously not all the time but to integrate it somehow with my commitments to the BBKA'.

'How much time are we looking at here, give me some sort of clue' said Piers.

'Well BIBBA have made a very preliminary enquiry and they wondered if I could go to Cornwall, say two days a month'.

'Two days a month, that doesn't sound very much does it, I personally would be happy to release you for two days a week which would be far more realistic. You could travel down on Sunday and return on Wednesday, two days with BIBBA and two days with us. I assume Richard that they would be funding you for your research work with them'.

'Oh yes of course and I can't see how it would be detrimental to my virus work, it really seems quite appropriate in some ways for me to be involved with both angles of what is a complex situation'.

The room fell silent as they both digested the facts and figures of their conversation until Piers stood up and reached out to shake hands with Richard. 'You will have a big workload Richard but I really can't think of anyone better to do it than you'.

'Thank you Piers, I won't let you down or BIBBA come to that' he replied.

'At the rate your going I can see you in the New Year's Honours List for your contribution to mankind'. Richard gave a small smile and thought to himself that perhaps he could too, standing on the steps of Buckingham Palace in a top hat and morning suit with Susan on his arm in a fetching outfit from some top London designer. After gathering his papers together he left the room and Piers in a very thoughtful mood looking out of his window onto the car park below.

I am going to be busy thought Richard and hoped that Susan would be alright with this new arrangement. He would tell her that it was only for a while and they would both have to live with it. Back in the office he saw that it was lunch time as George Myers tucked into a huge baguette with a rather suspicious looking filling. 'What the hell is that your eating' said Richard as he walked by.

'Grilled vegetables with pesto and mozzarella, Lisa said this is far more healthy than some of the junk I have been eating lately, I don't want to end up with one of those coronaries at my age' he replied.

Richard thought about the curry they had eaten on Friday night and the ominous greasy stain on the side of the bag and although he didn't agree with George on a lot of things he did on this. 'Good for you I'm sure that none of us want to end up just another statistic'.

Back at his desk Richard sat for a few moments taking stock of everything and now that his meeting was out of the way his thoughts turned to the next project. Over the weekend despite the upheaval at home he had gone over and over in his mind about the Professor and taking him into his confidence and Richard hoped, with the Professor's agreement a trip together. He would leave sharp at 4 o'clock and go to the library where he would invite the Professor to dinner, tomorrow night if possible as this really couldn't wait any longer.

At half past four Richard quickly made his way up the stairway in the library and through the archway spotted the Professor in conversation with a fellow colleague about finding a home for a large pile of books that were stacked on a trolley. While he waited he wondered over to the bottom shelf where the Professor had procured those books for him on his first visit and noted that the thickly bound Levens guide was still there.

'Richard what a nice surprise' said the Professor who now joined him and looked down at the shelf, 'I see you are still pursuing your historical enquiry with the monks at Fountains Abbey'.

'Yes I am but that's not what I'm here for Professor, my wife has deserted me for the next two weeks, family business you know and I wondered if you would join me for dinner one night, I always feel we have so much to talk about'. The professor reached out to straighten some books and turned to Richard.

'That would be delightful, I don't get out that much and it would be a change for me as well and as you so rightly say a chance to finish a lot of conversations we seem to have started but never finished'.

'What about tomorrow night, a bit short notice I know'.

'That is fine with me, just let me have your address and what time you want me'.

'Would 7.30 pm be alright, not too early for you'.

'No that's perfect and I will look forward very much to our evening together'.

'Oh just one more thing is there anything you don't eat'.

'No nothing apart from tripe'.

'Ugh me too such a disgusting mess. I will cook my speciality dish for you, chilli prawns with basil on a bed of linguine'.

'It sounds delightful' said the professor 'I can hardly wait'.

Richard patted the professor on his shoulder and as he turned to leave he looked back at the professor and replied 'No neither can I'.

Chapter Twenty

The following morning Richard brushed his teeth and mentally went through his list of priorities for the day. First of all as soon as he got into the office he would ring Bob Jenkins at BIBBA and confirm that everything was in order, the only thing he would need to check was if it would be o.k. for him to be on their payroll two days a week and more importantly when could he start this mapping work. Secondly he needed to get print outs of all the data relating to the Kashmir Bee Virus and lastly go to the supermarket and get the shopping for dinner that evening. After one final brush and a quick glance in the mirror Richard quickly grabbed his car keys and shut the front door behind him.

Despite Richard's earlier misgivings about him working eight days a month and not just the two as originally discussed, Bob Jenkins was delighted at the news and told Richard that it meant they would be able to complete this mapping work earlier than anticipated and that in the greater scheme of things the overall savings to the environment would far outweigh any additional costs. The only thing that Richard needed to let him know was how did he feel about travelling to Cornwall and would that be a problem for him to which Richard replied that it wouldn't.

Bob Jenkins briefly told him that the area he would be responsible for was St Justin-Roseland, a small hamlet located on the St. Mawes point. He had already contacted the Victory Inn, a small delightful pub right on the coastline in St. Mawes and reserved a double room that the proprietor was told would be required for an indefinite period, he would just need to confirm the details.

Finally Richard was told that everything would be put in writing and to look out for a large bundle of information in the post over the next couple of days that would explain all to him. He really knew nothing about BIBBA except that they were originally known as the Village Bee Breeders Association (VBBA) and were formed in 1964 by Beowulf Cooper who was an entomologist employed by the Ministry of Agriculture Fisheries and Food. He hoped that he had not bitten off more than he could chew but was confident that armed with his brief from BIBBA and, the promise of an assistant who would initially help him, felt sure that all would work out well.

Richard turned his printer on and watched as it churned out pages of information on the Kashmir Bee Virus that he would need for his conversation with the Professor later on. He didn't quite know how it would fit in with things but just knew that it was all part of what was going to happen. A shiver went down his spine, was he doing the right thing by involving the Professor, well whatever the outcome he would know within the next six hours or so. He had already decided that if the Professor was receptive to his revelations a trip would be made by them later in the week, he had to take every opportunity available to him in Susan's absence. Another thing he needed to sort out was the bee venom and particularly on his long trips to Cornwall. Would it be possible to somehow retrieve the venom and put it into a syringe, it would be so much more practical than transporting the bees.

'Richard I've just come off the phone from Bob Jenkins and it seems everything is pretty much in place, he was talking about you starting this mapping next week which is fine with me' said Piers who had now arrived at his desk.

'Yes that's great, I can't wait to get started'.

'What's all this stuff your printing' said Piers as he looked at the huge pile of sheets now sitting in the printer tray.

'Oh just getting on with as much as I can before I disappear next week' replied Richard.

'Good, well I'll leave you to it'.

In the supermarket some 40 minutes later Richard grabbed a basket and made his way to the fish counter where he procured a large bag of fresh king prawns plus a few other ingredients and finally completed the rest of his shopping with a pot of fresh basil. At the checkout he heard the operator inform him that he owed £15.20 as he placed his card into the automatic system and tapped in his pin number. He hoped that the Professor would enjoy his meal but wondered if it would in fact come second place bearing in mind the conversation that he was going to be having with him later on.

At exactly 7.30 pm the front door bell rang and Richard opened the door to a very smartly dressed Professor with a very fine looking bottle of Chablis that he placed in Richard's hands.

'I knew you were cooking seafood and thought this would go rather nicely with it'

'Yes it will, that's very kind of you'.

'What a lovely house you have Richard, Victorian yes'. Richard nodded in response and said that he would give him the guided tour and he had one particular room that he thought would be of interest to him and in that he was not wrong. He saved it till last and the Professor gave a small gasp as Richard swung the door open to his laboratory.

'It's simply charming Richard and has such great atmosphere'.

'You can feel it too, it was a chapel originally and the records show that a Reverend Bates lived here, the house was a presbytery you know'. The professor looked around the room and admiringly ran his hands over the fine high coloured tiles on the wall.

'You say you have only recently moved here'.

'Yes soon after New Year and I've got quite a lot of work to do on the property, when I find the time that is but nothing will be touched in here'.

'And I see from all your equipment that it is now a laboratory, for your bee viruses'.

'Yes the Kashmir Bee Virus, that is my forte and I'm shortly to start work on bee mapping in Cornwall with BIBBA, the plan is to find these wild bees and reintroduce them to the commercial hives'.

'My you are a busy man, my life by comparison is very staid, the library has its moments of course'.

'But what about your Quantum Mechanics and History doctorates, do you still lecture'.

'No not any longer, I used to but those days have long gone. But I must say that our acquaintanceship has opened things up a bit for me with our discussions.' Richard looked at the Professor who was now peering out of the lower stained glass window.

'Yes and I feel we have so much more to discuss' said Richard. 'Anyway I am falling down as a host Professor, what about a drink, sherry o.k..'

In the kitchen Richard topped up their glasses and gave a final stir to the linguine that now bubbled happily alongside the king prawns and basil. 'I always think this is such a healthy meal, pasta and fish with none of your saturated fats. You look as if you eat carefully though'.

The Professor laughed 'I have always been this size no matter what I eat, I'm one of the lucky ones with a high metabolic rate, I just burn up the calories'.

'Well I'll serve you a large portion and a smaller one for me' said Richard as he placed two large white bowls on the kitchen table and after pouring the Chablis sat down opposite the Professor. 'Bon appetite my friend'.

Richard had thought about when he would broach the subject and had decided that he would just say it, no big preamble just straight in at the deep end. As he twisted some particularly long strands of pasta on his fork and in the most casual way he said. 'I've travelled back in time you know'. He looked up from his fork and saw the Professor looking at him with an incredulous expression on his face.

'Excuse me I thought I just heard you say that you have travelled back in time'. The silence was deafening and you could have heard a pin drop.'

'Yes I have Professor, that was the reason for my conversation with you about quantum mechanics. You know that day when you asked if my interest in time travel was connected to the 12th century and Fountains Abbey, well it was because you see that's where I've been'. Some few minutes passed before the Professor took a very large mouthful of wine and said to Richard.

'You surely don't expect me to believe that you actually went back in time do you Richard'. He looked at him in total disbelief and shock.

'I know I know and also after having talked to you about the impossibility of travelling backwards in time it seems impossible, but it's not and I have'.

The Professor pushed his bowl of pasta to one side and sat with his hands clasped together in front of him and stared into space. 'Another drink' said Richard as he topped up their glasses and waited in silence for whatever was going to happen next.

'So how do you travel backwards, what happens'.

Richard thought for a few moments before he said 'I'll start at the beginning shall I. About four weeks ago, was it only four weeks it seems much longer than that somehow' he paused and took a breath 'Four weeks ago in my laboratory I was stung by a bee, one of my Kashmiri Virus bees when I was conducting an experiment. It was all so strange really, anyhow I was stung and that was when I first noticed that everything was different. You remember the stained glass window you looked out of earlier, well before the sting I noticed from the reflection by the moon on the wall from that window that it was a wild blustery night and immediately afterwards it was different and a calm silent one. But it didn't end there, when I went to find the door back into the passageway it was gone and instead I was standing in the warming house at Fountains Abbey, back in the 12th century'. He looked at the Professor who was now staring at him. 'How did I know it was the 12th century, well there was a blazing fire in the hearth and two figures were sat in front of it, one dressed as a monk and the other a lay brother and what's more I was totally invisible to them'. Richard stopped and looked at the Professor who had not moved. 'I spoke to them but they could not see me and I also witnessed the age old art of blood letting. Finally when I left the warming house and looked out of the door onto the quadrangle I saw Fountains Abbey in all its glory, not just as some ruin today but with all its buildings complete. And how did I return to the present day, it was when my wife Susan placed her hand on my shoulder'. The silence was electrifying and broken eventually by the Professor who said to Richard.

'And all this was substantiated by the Levens Guide that day in the library'.

'Yes it verified the historical events that I was witness to, the people, the conversations, the politics of the day, everything'.

The professor reached for a handkerchief in his top pocket and removed his spectacles to wipe his glasses in what seemed an almost physcological act as if he was trying to clear his vision. 'I remember you told me that it was the late 12th century you were interested in, what year was it when you went back'.

'It was 1185, the Springtime. Since then I've been back a number of times and on my last visit a few days ago the time difference seemed to change between now and then, I left here in April but it was mid Summer back there. I know the exact date on one of the trips though'. Richard stopped briefly and then continued. 'You know the day I came in with my face badly cut, well that was caused by the earthquake on the 15th April 1185'. I was in pursuit of Adolphus and Conan, they were the two people I originally encountered on my first visit by the fireside in the warming house and they always seem to be there when I go back. Adolphus is a monk and chief bee keeper, do you think he is my alter ego in another time, strange isn't it. Conan is a lay brother, a grange master. I was following them across the cloister when the earthquake struck and it brought me back to the present day and a nasty fall onto some of the large foundation stones, incredible isn't it.

'Richard I'm at a total loss as to what's happened, maybe your suffering from hallucinations. If you have managed to travel back in time then it goes against every law there is, I know there is vague talk about going forward in time but as I explained to you that day in the library to go back means travelling faster than the speed of light, do you truly believe you have done that'.

Richard sat down and shrugged his shoulders. 'All I know is that I have gone back and in line with what I have read in the library and seen on my computer these events that I have witnessed have been verified, every single one of them.

CHAPTER TWENTY-ONE

Richard looked at the congealed pasta in the bowls, long since forgotten and emptied them both out into the bin by the sink. A strange silence pervaded, not because there was nothing to say but because there was so much to say.

'I want you to tell me about the other trips you have made, down to every last detail' said the Professor.

'O.k. but let's go into the sitting room, we'll be more comfortable there'. Richard went to the drinks cabinet but the Professor discouraged him from drinking any more, he wanted if possible a sober reliable account of everything that had happened with nothing left out as it might be of vital importance. Some twenty minutes later Richard sat back in his chair and waited for the Professor to say something.

'You say that you are invisible to them, you can see your body but they can't' said the Professor.

'Yes that's right, when the King looked through the window I thought he could see me but instead of him staring at me it was Susan, it was almost hysterical in a way'.

'And your wife knows nothing about any of this and you've said nothing to anybody else'.

Richard shook his head but added that Susan was becoming suspicious of something but she wasn't sure what, an affair he probably thought.

'So on every occasion when you have gone back in time it's been after a bee sting.'

'Yes, whether it would happen if the sting was from an ordinary bee, by that I mean one not affected by this Kashmir Bee Virus I don't know. I've got a load of data I have compiled on this venom, would you like to see it'.

'Yes although it won't mean much to me, I'm not a scientist but nonetheless let me see it'. Some considerable time lapsed as the Professor read through the information and Richard could do nothing but wait in silence. Eventually after leafing backwards and forwards a few times the Professor looked up at Richard's expectant face. 'There's so much here I don't really understand but the crux of it as far as I can make out is, and I see you have underlined it here, how does Apitoxin with Melittin react to Dicistroviridae, does this cocktail become an hallucinogenic drug. We can sit and mull it over all night but I don't see how there is any conclusion we can come to'.

This was now the moment that Richard had waited for, the rest was just the lead up to it, a pathway to the inevitable. 'Professor there is one way that I can prove to you everything I have said, we could take a trip together'. He couldn't bring himself to look at the Professor and looked out of the French doors instead at a bird going through the motions of swallowing a very long worm that was making a bid for freedom but to no avail.

'Take a trip with you' the words were uttered as silently as a prayer by the graveside.

'Yes, then you will see that I am not imagining, not hallucinating' he paused 'I just want the chance to prove it and this is the only way possible, please Professor'.

'Richard I think I should go home now, I can't give you an answer not now. I need to think about it and let you know'.

Richard was disappointed and frustrated but understood that he needed time to decide. 'Because my wife is away I want us to do this trip in the next day or so, it's a perfect opportunity with the house empty. It's important that we have somewhere safe as every time I have taken a trip outdoors it seems to end in disaster'. The Professor stared at Richard. 'That night I was in the restaurant and then that day at Fountains Abbey, there are just too many people and too many questions'.

'I will ring you tomorrow, in the afternoon and let you know'.

Richard went to the front door and watched as the Professor carefully closed the front gate behind and after a small waive disappeared down the road. He felt fretful, anxious, what had he done. He wondered if a van with men in white coats would shortly be knocking on his door to take him away but thought probably not. The Professor was an intellectual, a doctor twice over and therefore needed the space to go over things in his mind and come to some sort of decision. He decided to ring Susan and see how she was getting on, not particularly because he was interested in the latest situation her end but because he simply needed to hear another human voice and, especially one unconnected with this evening.

After five minutes on the phone he almost wished he hadn't bothered as Susan went through a list of her activities since she arrived including the menus that the patient had consumed. As Susan came to the end of her conversation she asked Richard if he was alright as he sounded very tired. After reassuring her that all was fine and he loved her, he replaced the receiver in its cradle. He had meant to tell her about Cornwall but with everything going round his head had totally forgotten, never mind he thought to himself as that seemed the least of his worries at this moment in time. Tomorrow was all he could think about, he made sure the Professor had all his telephone numbers, the office, home and mobile and he could now do nothing but wait. Back in the kitchen he busied himself with washing up and clearing the kitchen going through the conversation he had had earlier in his head, he hoped liked a barrister in court that he had given a good delivery and a concise presentation of the facts but there was little more he could do now, it was all in the lap of the gods so to speak.

Sleep came eventually after Richard tossed and turned for what seemed like hours to him and when he did drop off he had the strangest dream. He had gone back twenty years ago to when he had first met Susan and, being the dutiful son that he was soon invited her home to meet his parents. They took to Susan just as he had but on one of her visits in the kitchen over a cup of tea he was questioned about these trips he took. His father, a staunch traditional Catholic, said it was a sin to mess with dark forces and he would surely go to hell and Susan said it frightened her and that unless he ceased immediately with the trips she could never marry him. Richard suddenly woke with a pounding heart and sweat pouring down his face, God what a nightmare he thought. He lay quietly for a few moments and then pulled back the duvet cover and got out of bed.

Downstairs in the kitchen he made himself a cup of tea and saw that it was only 3 'o clock and still the early hours of the morning. After a few sips he began to feel wide awake and knew that he would have done another trip there and then but all of the apis mellafera had gone, he craved an apis mellafera like a smoker craves a cigarette with an empty pack. How strange the dream was he thought to himself and wondered if subconsciously he felt guilty about not telling Susan what had happened, he had told the Professor who to be honest by comparison was a virtual stranger, but not Susan. And what about his father, was he suffering from some kind of deep rooted guilt about being a lapsed Catholic after the death of his father and the ensuing dark night of the soul. He would ask the Professor what he thought about it but now his eyelids had started to droop and, in comparison to some thirty minutes earlier felt exhausted. He climbed the stairs and got back into bed and found himself praying that the morning would soon come, and as far as he was concerned it couldn't come soon enough.

CHAPTER TWENTY-TWO

As it happened he didn't have to wait long for his answer when his mobile rang at 7.30 a.m. Richard didn't recognise the number and pressed a button to receive the call. 'It's me' a voice said in a quiet almost conspiratorial tone 'And the answer is yes. I have been awake most of the night thinking about it and I want to go ahead '. The phone now went silent.

Richard replied in a slow deliberate voice after a few moments. 'So you do believe me and that I am not just some sort of nutter'.

'I've thought about nothing else since I left you last night and not about you being a nutter either. If this is true it breaks all the laws of science, laws I have studied for decades and the empirical approach is all that is now left us to try and solve this mystery or, whatever else you may chose to call it.'

'So by going back with me and seeing it for yourself will in your own mind prove everything I have said'.

'Yes but what it proves really I am not sure, either that I am hallucinating like you or we have travelled in time, still in a way pure conjecture. I was thinking about the fact that you can see them but they can't see you'.

'And what do you think that means'.

'I'm not sure really. Might mean that it is just hallucinations'.

'So if they could see us and speak to us then it would be real'.

'Yes I suppose so, whatever real is in the circumstances'.

'Professor the question is when'.

The phone went silent until he heard the reply he had longed for 'Tonight Richard, I can scarcely function at the moment and dread the thought of having to wait any longer, tonight'.

'Yes tonight it is'. The conversation ended abruptly and Richard was left feeling like a prisoner in the dock awaiting the verdict of the jury, would he be proved right or wrong and he only had a few hours to wait now for the answer.

Richard's visit to the office was only a brief one purely to collect the apis mellafera. The office was quiet with the usual Wednesday morning meeting that he would normally have attended but with his new commitment to BIBBA was excused. In the laboratory he carefully opened the fridge door and started to fill the plastic container with the bees and was disturbed by one of the technicians who had now joined him.

'You're going through those bees like hot cakes Mr Fellowes, I can hardly keep up with your demand'. Richard stopped in his tracks and turned to look at him noticing that he possessed a massive shock of ginger hair and the most hideously freckled face.

'Yes yes I'm going through a particularly important part of the experiment at the moment so a plentiful supply is essential' he replied.

'If you so say'.

'Quite, well I'll not keep you I'm sure you have a lot to do'.

'Yes Mr Fellowes, I just have to update these graphs and I'll leave you in peace'.

He watched as the technician drew a few lines and then closed the door behind him. He shut the lid on the container that was now full of bees and the only other thing he needed was a syringe to simplify the stinging process. In a large drawer he found what he was looking for and pocketed two hypodermic needles complete with protective plastic caps. He removed one of them and looked at the dangerous looking instrument in his hand and hoped that he would be able to use it, but not yet he thought, it was first things first and at the moment it was a good supply of venom for his trip with the professor later on.

When Richard opened his front door back at home a large brown envelope lay on the mat that he immediately recognised as the information that he had been waiting for from BIBBA. Their logo was printed in large green letters with a bee sitting on top of the I instead of a dot, how clever he thought to himself. He placed the envelope on the hall table and made a mental note that he would deal with that tomorrow, but not today. In his laboratory Richard placed the container with the bees into the wooden box carefully pushing it to the back of the shelf. He checked his watch and saw that it was only 2 o'clock and therefore still a few agonising hours to wait before the Professor arrived. The telephone rang and Richard had a sudden terrible thought that it was the Professor ringing to say that his better judgement dictated and he would not do the trip. He hesitated as he lifted the receiver and it was with great relief that he heard Robyn's voice at the other end of the line.

'Dad how are you, mum rang me last night and said that I should come over for dinner tonight, is that alright'.

'Oh love I would normally have said yes but I have a friend coming over this evening, a rather elderly gentleman, a Professor and I think you would find it all rather dull and boring. Can we do tomorrow instead'.

'Yea no problem dad, I'll see you around 6'.

Richard stared at the silent receiver before replacing it in the cradle. With the ready supply of his apis mellafera he was tempted to do a trip but decided not to, he had never done two trips in a day before and didn't know if that would change anything and he wanted the conditions to be perfect for later. The silence of the house was driving him insane and he could settle to nothing, the television drove him mad and the radio became an incessant babble in the background. He then thought about Susan and was consumed with guilt as he had done nothing to the house since they moved in, there were numerous jobs to be done, painting, wallpapering and the downstairs loo needed attention as it frequently refused to flush without a great deal of coaxing. Be positive Richard told himself and decided that he would sort out some of the paint if nothing else, the wallpaper he would leave until Susan came home as that definitely would be a joint decision.

In his local DIY store Richard released one of the trolleys and began his journey around its cavernous interior lit by a myriad of spotlights. He wheeled past floor coverings, bathrooms, kitchens, wall coverings and eventually came to the paint section. He wouldn't get it all today as there was quite a lot that needed painting and he settled on Robyn's bedroom, she wanted some hideous purple and black colour scheme, quite gothic he thought to himself so purple it was. His eyes scoured the shelf until he had looked at every shade of purple there was and finally decided on a shade called quite appropriately he thought Bishops Frock. As he looked further up the shelf he noticed in the white section a paint called White Monk, he never knew that paints could be so religious. He just needed the black paint and settled on Shades of Night. After adding some brushes, undercoat and paint cleaner to his trolley Richard settled his account and wheeled his trolley out into the car park. He felt better now, at least he had made an effort and decided that he would make a start on Robyn's room tomorrow and then when she came for dinner she could give her seal of approval, hopefully.

Back in the driveway Richard lifted the tailgate and retrieved three large plastic carrier bags containing his purchases and once inside the house stored the various pots and bags in the corner of the hallway. As he turned to shut the door he noticed a figure standing on the front doormat, it was the Professor.

'I'm sorry but I've arrived far too early, I know we said tonight'.

Richard reached forward and shook the Professor's hand 'You don't have to say anything because you see I know what it's like, I understand'.

'Yes' he replied quietly.

'It was driving me mad, the waiting around so I went shopping, DIY shopping'.

The Professor looked at the decorating equipment spread around the hall floor and said 'Funny you don't strike me as a DIY man'

'I'm not replied' replied Richard, 'It's guilt really as Susan has been waiting so patiently for these jobs to be done'.

'And you haven't had the time' the Professor interjected.

'There never seems enough time, there's that word again' said Richard.

'Can I come in' said the Professor now turning his gaze towards Richard.

'Yes yes of course, forgive me, would you like a drink' said Richard.

'A cup of coffee thank you'.

In the kitchen Richard watched the water start to bubble in the kettle and waited for the switch to turn off at the side. 'I was thinking that we will go into the sitting room for out trip, it will be more comfortable than the laboratory and more space too'.

'Why do you think that we will need a lot of space' said the Professor.

'Well it's my first trip that I won't be solo'.

'Do you think that we will be able to see or touch each other'.

'I don't know but we will soon find out'.

They both drank their coffee in silence and then placed their drained cups in the sink. 'Does it ever bother you Richard about not being able to get back to the present'.

'No can't say it's something I think about, I suppose that when you are back there so much is happening. The transition in some ways is so quick, I mean going there and coming back, the return can be brought about by either a touch or a noise'. The Professor nodded gently and looked expectantly at Richard.

'It's time now, are you ready'. Go into the sitting room and I will fetch the bees'.

Richard put the box onto the coffee table and picked up his tweezers. Before he extracted one of the bees he thought out loud and said 'As you know it's my first trip with someone else so I don't know if we will end up in the same place as each other. I will inflict the sting on you first and then myself immediately afterwards'.

The Professor rolled up his sleeve and stretched his arm out 'Do it now' he said closing his eyes tightly. Richard grasped a bee and jabbed it into his arm and immediately completed the same process on himself. It felt as though the transition was immediate, the first thing Richard noticed was the colourful tapestry of the Garden of Eden hanging on the dark grey stone wall that he recognised, they had arrived back in the Abbot's quarters. He heard a voice behind him say 'I've made it, I'm here too Richard'. Looking round he saw the Professor sitting on the bed with a look of utter disbelief and amazement on his face. 'This is just unbelievable, unbelievable. I can see you Richard and you can see me too'.

'Yes I can'. He walked over and touched the Professor's arm that was clutching the side of the bed. 'Can you feel that'.

'Yes I can, where are we'.

'I was here once before on another trip, we're in the Abbot's quarters at Fountains Abbey'. Richard wanted to ask him about the transition, what it had felt like to him but knew that any conversation would have been futile at that moment as the Professor was so in awe of what had happened, it was a conversation they would have later. Any further talk between them ceased as they now heard a door open in the outer room followed by muffled voices. They both moved to the door and saw the King and Bishop Challoner now standing in silence looking at each other.

'Tis a sad day for Fountains sire, make no mistake' said the Bishop.

'The Abbot will not go quietly, of that I am sure'.

Richard remembered the words of Conan in the warming house on that first trip when he said that things could not carry on as they were, that the Abbot was bleeding their coffers dry by the day as well as massive loans from a Jewish financier. He looked at the King's fine attire and wondered if this was the equivalent of 12th century power dressing for the occasion. Around his neck was a chain and a fine ermine stole, Richard thought that he looked like a lion out for its prey and thought of the famous play The Lion in Winter by James Goldman, a purely fictional tale of course about Henry II and a family Christmas gathering at Chinon in 1183, to supposedly name his successor.

'Then we must make our case, and make it well' replied the Bishop. 'According to law and the authority vested in me I as Bishop can depose him and you as King can then give assent for his replacement'. The King nodded gently and looking at the Bishop said.

'You make it sound easy Bishop, too easy, take nothing for granted'.

The sound of shuffling footsteps could now be heard from the staircase and the door slowly opened to reveal the Abbot who looking at them both simply said 'I have been summoned'.

'Yes Abbot, be seated' said the Bishop pointing to a chair in the corner 'Don't look so worried, we are here to do our best for the abbey, and you' he added. The Abbot did not look very convinced and fussed with his robes as he settled himself in the chair.

The Bishop glanced at the King and then at the Abbot, 'I am sure you know that for some time things have been amiss financially, you have come to office some five years ago and the debt we have amassed is considerable, a vast fortune I have to say'. The Abbot looked at the Bishop and thought to himself that the abuse of hospitality they had suffered at the hands of the nobles, officials and royalty had done little to help.

'I have dismissed Jerome and Gower' said the Abbot in a defiant mood, 'They have both been banished'.

The Bishop sat next to him and placed his hand on the Abbot's shoulder. 'Yes those who chose to steal our silver and food, but it is too little too late, they were small fish to fry in our pan'. He stopped and cleared his throat. 'Our principal asset is wool and it has come to light that sacks have been sold in advance, whereby the abbey has contracted to sell home-grown wool, without coth, gard, black, grey, putrid scab, torn-off skin, grease, clact, bard, or bad skin, some 50,000 sacks to be exact over some four years'. A silence hung in the air that was broken at last by the Bishop 'We have been duty bound to pay a sum of £10 for every sack in default, that adds up to a tidy sum of £500'. He bent down and picked up a linen roll that was now placed on the table and untied the cord around its middle. 'Here we have the documents of your misdemeanour, your folly, call it what you will'. The Abbot's face turned grey as he looked at the manuscript in front of him and he went to speak but no words came out of his mouth. The Bishop briefly looked at the pages as he turned them until he came to the last one and ran his finger slowly down the yellow parched sheet. 'You made this pledge in the year of our Lord in 1181, the 5th July to be exact to the Italian merchant Francesto da Russo in Genoa, this is your signature is it not'. He pulled the sheet in front of the Abbot who nodded in consent.

'You have without my permission chosen to plunder my private library, how can this be' said the Abbot.

'Enough' said the King whose rudy complexion had now started to turn a deep shade of crimson. 'We are not here to discuss our actions, only yours and grim they are'.

'Abbot amongst this manuscript I am most distressed to see that you owe £500 to the Mayor of London as well as

£1,000 to one Robert de la Plante. All of these monies due are far in excess of the revenue of this abbey and thus we sink into a mire'. The Bishop picked the manuscript up and slowly rolled it together in his hands and retied the cord. 'My Abbot it is with sorrow that we now have the grave task of deposing you and your rule at Fountains. We will also need to make haste with our arrangements for not only your successor but also for you as well'

The Abbot now stood up and knelt before the King 'Sire I beg your leniency in this matter and beg that you forgive my failings and grant me another chance'. He paused slightly as he licked his quivering lips and continued. 'Sire could you see your way to granting a fair at the abbey gateway, with the revenue from the tolls and a proclamation from you that traders must not buy or sell within five miles other than at the fair, Dover and Chester have had such fairs much to their gain'. The King looked at the Bishop and then turned his gaze towards the Abbot.

'No Abbot I cannot, I will not permit any fair or suchlike, our decision is final'. The Abbot slowly stood up and returned to his chair in silence with tears that were now starting to well in his eyes and fall silently down his cheeks.

CHAPTER TWENTY-THREE

'*Mea culpas*' he said in a quiet hardly audible voice.

'What did you say Abbot, your fault, yes' said the Bishop.

'What will become of me now, I see that my days here are soon to be numbered, I have heard muttering of Henry Cuylter, your sacrist as being my successor'.

'Yes in that you are not wrong. He is not such a spiritual man as you are, indeed his talents lie in more worldly things' he paused slightly before adding 'in money to be short and that at the moment that is something much in demand, particularly at Fountains'.

'You have still not answered my question, what is to become of me'.

'The successor to Henry Cuylter will need an assistant, you are ripe for the picking'.

'Am I not only to be deposed but insulted too' said the Abbot wiping his eyes with a cloth.

'Humility brother, humility, walk with our God' said the Bishop. 'There are lessons to be learnt'.

'But too late for me I fear, you must not send me to York, I beg you to send me somewhere to see out my days, in quiet contemplation'.

'We are not that unforgiving Abbot, where is it that you believe you belong?'

The Abbot looked out of the window seemingly lost in thought until he said at some length 'I need somewhere quiet where I can be left in peace, to pray. Sire Lindisfarne Priory on the Holy Island, *Medicata* (*Insula*) the healing island is where I truly believe our Lord is calling me, my failings here at Fountains are but a pathway to that end'.

Richard looked at the Abbot who had now become a desperate figure clutching at straws and starting to look as though he was beginning to lose his marbles as he paced the floor wringing his hands together. 'St. Cuthbert was the bishop of Lindisfarne and I have heard he was a man of God, devoted to unceasing prayer and kindly to all'. He lowered his voice now and added almost in a whisper 'he performed miracles too'.

There are many coincidences in life Richard thought to himself as he remembered a visit just some three or four weeks ago to Durham Cathedral, a magnificent edifice to the Norman Romanesque style with a touch of Byzantine. He had marvelled at the massive spiral zig zag columns that lined the nave and the huge rose window in the chapel of the nine altars. At the back of the cathedral to one side Richard had found the tomb of St. Cuthbert cited just behind the high altar, an almost modest affair covered with grey stone and simply marked with the name *Cuthbertus*.

'Sire I will take my leave now and hurry to prayer' said the Abbot. He paused slightly at the door before he went adding 'to St. Cuthbert'. With a small bow he left the King and the Bishop who stared at each other with an expression of almost disbelief.

'I am sure he is going quite mad' said the Bishop shaking his head 'will you make presentations to Lindisfarne for him'.

'Tis not a matter that I take to my heart or I deem important' said the King.

The Bishop ran his fingers along the edge of the table in thought 'Do you believe Sire that he will go quietly or oppose us and fight his claim in court'.

'I am not sure but it may well be on reflection that Lindisfarne could be our panacea, Fountains will then be but just a dim memory for him, remember I am King so my wishes have to be acquiesced. I shall despatch one of my courtiers to the Holy Island forthwith and put arrangements in place'.

'A wise decision Sire, with much to do a legal wrangle is not desirable'.

Richard felt a tug on his sleeve and turned to the Professor who was some six feet away, something was happening. He instinctively stretched out and reached for the Professor's arm and watched as the backdrop of the grey stone walls was replaced by the patterned wallpaper of his sitting room wall. Richard blinked his eyes and saw Robyn standing in front of him with a look of horror on her face. 'Dad, dad, what's going on'.

Richard gathered himself together and looked to see the Professor who was now sitting in an armchair wiping his brow. 'Nothing is wrong Robyn, I told you that the Professor was coming tonight and that we would be busy with things'.

'What things, that's I want to know. When I came in you were both' Robyn paused slightly 'you were both looking at something but I don't know what, it was in the corner of the room but I couldn't see anything'.

Richard knew what she meant and also what she possibly could not know. They had been eavesdropping on a conversation some 800 years ago back in the mists of time between a King, a Bishop and a deposed Abbot. 'I didn't think that you were coming round tonight, remember I said we were going to be busy experimenting'.

'But experimenting what dad, you both looked so strange, so odd' said Robyn.

Richard looked at the Professor and then back at Robyn 'let me introduce you to Professor Durnley, PhD Quantam Mechanics no less'. Not forgetting her manners Robyn reached out and shook hands with the Professor.

'And I hear that you are an up and coming young dance star' said the Professor in an attempt to defuse the situation.

'Yes but I have a long way to go before I realise my dreams' she replied. 'But you still haven't said what you were doing'.

'It really would take so long to explain, really it would, but Robyn don't mention this to your mother, you know how she worries about me' said Richard. She looked at her father for a few moments before turning on her kneel and making her way to the sitting room door.

"I'll see you tomorrow night dad, on your own though' as she cast a somewhat disparaging glance at the Professor 'bye'.

They both heard the front door bang and Richard looked at the Professor. 'I'm sorry about that, she is quite highly strung you know, her artistic bent'.

'Don't worry Richard, remember I have children too, as well as grandchildren' he added.

Richard glanced at the Professor and said in a gentle voice 'quite'.

The professor dropped into an armchair and looked at Richard for a few moments in silence. 'You know I still have contacts within the University and I have spoken to an old colleague of mine, not in my department I hasten to add but in toxicology'. He paused for a few moments before continuing. 'I discussed this mixture of apitoxin with dicistroviridae and the results were quite alarming'. Richard looked at the Professor in silence.

'You haven't told him about this have you'.

'No, nothing, I can assure you that your secret is safe with me but I won't be doing any more trips with you'.

Richard looked at the Professor with a totally deflated expression, 'Was that trip really your first and last one, please don't say it was'.

'This mixture Richard is lethal, I mean in the normal course of events you may be stung once and that to all intents and purposes would be that with little or no harmful effects, but you are ingesting this stuff in huge amounts and in short poisoning yourself'. Richard fell silent for a while and at length drew a deep breath.

'I think there may be a way round it'.

The Professor stood up and took a few steps round the floor 'And what is that'.

'Well up to now I have always used a bee and received the venom by jabbing it into my arm as I did just now. If you could use a syringe to extract the venom I could use smaller amounts for each trip and could control my intake but I don't know of course if that would affect the trip. As a matter of fact I had already decided to use a syringe instead of the conventional method so to speak as my arms are starting to look like those of a junkie with sores and horrible looking scabs'. He rolled up his sleeve and turned his arm towards the Professor 'You see what I mean'.

'Richard you shouldn't be using this stuff, this venom in any quantity, please listen to me'. He looked at Richard and saw that his words had had little or no effect as he peered at the glazed expression in his eyes and thought to himself that this was a dead man walking, that was the phrase they used on death row wasn't it he thought to himself, for those whose fate was sealed.

'On my next trip I will use a syringe, if your interested I'll let you know how it goes' said Richard in an almost disinterested way.

'Richard I hope that we can still be friends, I hope that you will still visit me at the library, I shall always be pleased to see you but I can't be any part of this'.

'Yes' said Richard quietly as he pulled the curtains on a rapidly descending nightfall 'I hope too that we can remain friends despite what has happened today'.

'I think it's time I left' said the Professor as he made his way to the hall and reached for the catch on the front door. 'Take care of yourself Richard'.

'Yes I will' he replied as he watched him disappear up the front path and the quiet click of the front gate behind him. Back in the house a deep silence prevailed, an almost deafening silence that made him want to shout but he was left on his own with the echoing words of the Professor in his ears that he was poisoning himself, could that be possible he thought. A sharp shivering sensation went down his spine and, to accompany it, a terrible sense of doom, the most awful dreadful sense of impending doom.

Chapter Twenty-Four

The next morning Richard stared at the large brown envelope in his hand from BIBBA and then at the DIY bags that were still sitting in the corner of the hall. He had to get a grip he told himself, there was really so much to do and his first priority was BIBBA. He remembered that it was only a couple of days before he was off to Cornwall and he hadn't spoken to Susan yet about this new work arrangement either. He opened the flap of the envelope and pulled out a large handfull of papers that included a magazine, some brochures, a thickly bound volume of typewritten notes, a map and lastly a handwritten letter.

'Dear Richard,

I have taken the liberty of writing to you rather than phoning and will start by introducing myself. I'm Justin Blake and will be your working partner in Cornwall over the next few months, or indeed however long it takes to complete our task. I'm not sure how much Bob Jenkins has filled you in on bee mapping so have enclosed some fairly comprehensive notes that I hope will answer some if not most of your questions.

Accommodation has been reserved for you at the Victory Inn in St. Mawes, can I suggest that we meet there at around midday this Sunday, if that's not convenient please just let me know.

Looking forward to meeting you and what I hope will be a successful venture together.

Yours Justin Blake

Amongst the paperwork was a flyer from the Victory Inn that Richard now held in his hand reliably informing him of accommodation and food that was second to none. He tapped in the telephone number of the establishment and waited a few moments until he heard a very deep gravely voice at the other end of the line.

'Jim Mates at your service, how can I help you'

'Oh good morning, I'm Richard Fellowes and understand that you have a booking in my name over the coming months'.

'Just a jiffy I need to get the accommodation book and I'll be with you'. Richard fiddled with the flex on the telephone while he waited and thought that he must ring Susan after he had finished this call.

'Yes I have your booking Mr Fellowes, it was made by BIBBA, is that correct'.

'Yes, the Bee Improvement and Bee Breeders Association'.

'If you say so sir, so when can we expect you'.

'Well the normal arrangement would be for me to stay with you for three nights during the week, Sunday to Tuesday and then I would travel back home on the Wednesday morning'.

'No problem, we've reserved a nice double room for you at the front of the hotel looking out over the sea, it's very popular and our regular guests always ask if it's available'.

'Then I'm sure that I will be happy too'. Richard paused slightly. 'As this is my first visit I wanted to come down a bit earlier to get things set up so am wondering if on this occasion I can stay with you from the Friday night'. He heard the rustle of paper as Jim Mates consulted his book and was told there was no problem and they would look forward to seeing him then.

There then followed the dutiful telephone call to Susan during which he told her about Cornwall and much to his surprise met with no resilience whatsoever. She told him that it would not be for ever and no need to worry. Richard did worry then as this was the second occasion when he had announced his absence to which she was totally acquiescent, perhaps she was just getting used to it he thought but decided that when this was all over, the visits to Cornwall as well as the trips, he was going to concentrate on his marriage and Susan. Perhaps they could take a long holiday somewhere, yes they would do that.

Whilst his thoughts were on travel he checked out his train route for Cornwall using the journey planner with British Rail and quickly jotted down on a notepad that from Durham Central he would go straight down to King's Cross, make his way across London to Paddington Station and then get a direct train to Truro. Once he was local he could make the short trip by car for about the last 40 minutes to St. Mawes. It certainly wasn't a short journey and would take him some 10 hours or more and calculated that he would need to be on a train out of Durham around 9 a.m. in the morning. He tore the page off the pad and put it in the large brown envelope with all the rest of the information from BIBBA and turned his thoughts to the rest of the day. He would need to visit the office and tidy his desk in view of his forthcoming absence, as well as of course obtain the relevant supply of bee venom that he would now inject into his arm via syringe. He remembered the slim surgical case in the top drawer of his dressing table in the bedroom upstairs that contained the two syringes he had obtained from the laboratory at work and thought that he must not forget to pack them. Richard planned to take a trip on the Saturday morning as he had a free day until he met with Justin Sunday lunchtime and, as always, savoured the prospect. The telephone rang and he half wondered if the professor had called to say that he had changed his mind but it was Robyn on the other end of the line who said she was going to bring some KFC in for dinner that evening as she wanted to save him from the bother of cooking.

In the office Richard quickly checked his post and made sure that he had everything he needed for Cornwall which just left the most important thing of all the bees. He had just finished a phone call to one of his colleagues when he spotted George Myers making his way over to his desk and he gave an inward grimace. 'Who's top of the class then, lucky man' said George as he propped himself on the edge of Richard's desk.

'Oh what's that then' replied Richard.

'Your secondment to BIBBA of course with nice trips to Cornwall every week'.

Richard eyed him slowly and replied 'Yes and a lot of work too plus many hours travelling'.

'If you say so, of course it might be just another way of giving you a bit of a holiday'.

'How's that' said Richard who was starting to get annoyed with him.

'After your funny little turn at the conference the other week, it was all the talk you know'.

Richard now stood up and looked at his face wishing that he could punch his lights out, the annoyance had now gone and was replaced with sheer anger. Luckily for George the moment was saved as Piers who had overhead their exchange called over and told him that he had a job for him. George slowly lifted himself from the desk and gave a sly grin before disappearing with Piers out of the office. Richard took a couple of deep breaths and knew that he had to get out of there as soon as possible and after collecting his bees made his way back to his car and then home.

Robyn arrived at around 6 o'clock armed with a bucket of KFC and the news that she had been selected to represent her dance class at a competition in Dortmund next month. She simply had to go she told Richard as it would be wonderful and could he pay the deposit for £100 straight away. He smiled at her youthful enthusiasm and told her he was very proud and yes of course she must go whatever the cost. After dinner during which she had regaled him with every last bit of information about the competition, Richard loaded the dishwasher and afterwards wandered into the hall where Robyn was staring at the DIY bags in the corner.

'What's all this' she said flicking open the top of one of the bags.

'I'm going to make a start on the decorating and I've got all the stuff for your room. You said you wanted gothic so I hope you'll like the purple and black colour scheme'.

'Cool dad, it looks great' she said 'When are you going to make a start'.

'Soon, soon Robyn' although he wondered how soon what with Cornwall now. Richard was glad that no mention was made of the incident with the Professor and the evening drew to a close as he waived goodbye to her shortly after 8 o'clock Upstairs in the bedroom Richard pulled a large holdall from the top of a wardrobe and filled it with his overnight things plus some waterproofs for his outdoor work as well as some smart slacks and a few shirts and jumpers, he hoped that he had packed enough but could use this trip as a dry run for the future. Finally he opened the top drawer of his dressing table and grasped a slim blue box that held the two syringes, he released the catch at the front and lifted the lid to see them carefully nestled between some tissue paper and thought that yes it would also be their dry run too.

CHAPTER TWENTY-FIVE

The 9.20 a.m. train from Durham to King's Cross slowly pulled away from platform ten exactly on time. After depositing his holdall in the overhead rack Richard settled himself back into his seat and was pleased to see that the train was half empty and a perfect opportunity for him to read his notes from BIBBA about bee mapping or bee lining as it was also known. There were a number of suspected locations for the black honeybee from Scotland to Ireland, Wales and the West Country to which Richard was now headed and he was quietly confident that Justin Blake would be able to fill him in on any of the gaps he might have.

Out of the window he watched the grey city disappear into an urban sprawl and then eventually give way to the green open space of the countryside. He pondered on the idea that there were grey people and green people, he was not thinking of any ageing portion the population or those environmentally conscious, he was thinking about how poles apart mentally the city dwellers and the country dwellers were and what different lives they led. The green people clung to the past and the grey people to the future, whatever that may be. He heard somebody clear their throat and looked up to see an elderly gentleman hovering over the seat opposite him.

'Is this seat free' he enquired peering at Richard.

'Yes, I'm quite alone here'.

'Thank you, I thought it probably was but just wanted to check'.

Richard nodded silently and turned back to his BIBBA paperwork conscious of a rumbling stomach. It had been a very early start, too early for sandwiches and hence no lunch. He stood up to make his way to the buffet car but was stopped in his tracks as his travelling companion suddenly said 'Well what a strange coincidence'.

'What's that' said Richard sitting down again.

'Well I couldn't help noticing your paperwork about bees, I used to keep them until this dammed arthritis took over'. He looked down at his hands saying 'They are useless and good for nothing these days'. Richard looked down at his hands and then back to his face.

'I'm sorry to hear that'.

'Yes I had many hives and was always a most active member of the local Bee Society, until this' he said. 'But please I am most interested, tell me about yourself and the bees' he added. Richard had dreaded the thought of any interruptions but now found this a most welcome one.

'Let me introduce myself, I'm Richard Fellowes and work for the BBKA but am currently on secondment to BIBBA'.

'You've no need to explain either of those organisations as I know everything there is to know about bees'. He stood up and held out his hand 'David Squires'. Richard returned the handshake and now studied the face of his travelling companion at close quarters noticing that he had small dark coloured beady eyes and a nose that seemed to twitch, he thought to himself that if you could have just added a set of whiskers he would have looked like a mouse.

'Of course if this dammed arthritis' he heard him say 'Hadn't struck how much more I could have done, how much more I could have achieved'. Richard gently nodded his head to and fro silently sympathising with him.

'Yes life can be cruel can't it'.

'Tell me more about your secondment' said David.

'Well', said Richard taking a breath, 'We are hoping with this bee mapping to re-introduce the black bee and in short save the bee population and its terrible decline'.

'Although my hands are useless my eyes aren't and I have been following the latest developments very closely in this regard. Most people are totally unaware of its vital importance to us and our food chain, also the amazing fact that bees are the only animal, albeit wild animal, that make food for humans, quite extraordinary isn't it'.

Richard's stomach was no longer just rumbling but starting to growl now as well, 'You must excuse me I need to find the buffet car and some food'.

'I think that's where you were off to before I intercepted you' said David pulling a rather old and dilapidated rucksack onto his lap. 'I've brought my own with me, just plain cheese and pickle, I have to be careful you know as some of this commercial food is full of additives that really plays havoc with my digestion'.

'I won't be long, can I get you anything'. David shook his head and took a large bite out of his sandwich. 'By the way where are you going to'.

'Cromer to stay with my sister for a week or two and also to enjoy the excellent seafood, particularly crab which I am most pleased to say I can eat'. Richard did a quick calculation in his head and knew that his travelling companion would be getting off at Peterborough, the large cathedral city that lay east of the massive area of fens and marshlands.

'You are going to Norfolk and will be one of the North folk'. David stopped eating and looked at Richard. 'If you were going to Suffolk you would be one of the South folk'. He paused, it's a remnant of the ancient Anglo Saxon Kingdom you know, the East Angles'.

Richard left David who was just about to tuck into another sandwich and walked the length of three carriages till he came to the buffet car. There was a bit of a queue and Richard leaned back against the carriage wall swaying gently back and forth with the motion of the train as he watched the small towns and villages slip by effortlessly en-route to the great metropolis. His turn soon came and he ordered a large coffee and a bacon and sausage roll with brown sauce from a very helpful and attentive caterer. After handing over what Richard considered to be an extortionate amount of money he made his way back to the carriage where he found David fast asleep with his arms wrapped around the rucksack. He didn't blame him, you couldn't be too careful especially these days. He sat back to enjoy his breakfast and read a little more of his notes and after some length looked up to see the unmistakeable twin towers of York Minster come into view. Even at this distance you could see it was a huge magnificent edifice, but more importantly Richard knew that some just some twenty miles the other side of it lay Fountains Abbey and he thought of the monks, especially Adolphus and Conan who were back there 800 years ago in the grey mists of time. He wondered if David knew about medieval bee keeping and their crude hives that were no more than wicker baskets plastered together with mud and dung, not forgetting of course the amazing stone hives carved into the pinnacles. How he wished that he could have shared them with him but knew that he never could and was a lone solitary traveller in space and time.

'You look far away' he heard a voice say and looked up to see that his travelling companion had now stood up and was busy brushing the numerous crumbs of the front of his jacket.

'Yes I was just thinking about the bees as usual and the irony of life'.

'What irony is that' said David who had now extracted an ancient looking flask from his rucksack and had commenced pouring a very strong looking cup of coffee, it was nearly black with just a fleck of milk, it was he thought the equivalent of builder's tea, was there such a thing as builder's coffee he thought.

'That we humans, civilized supposedly, with all our trappings of modernity and inventions could come to rely on such a tiny little thing as a bee, it's quite extraordinary really and in many ways a quite humbling moment'.

'And do you think there is some kind of moral to this story' said David taking another sip of his coffee.

Richard thought for a few moments and looked up at him 'I believe that however superior we humans believe ourselves to be, we always have a master' he paused slightly here and looked upward pointing a finger 'I'm not talking about a deity here but nature who sometimes is relentless with her tsunami's and earthquakes, we are really quite powerless it seems'.

David had finished his coffee and was wiping the cup out with a tissue 'I agree with you Richard, all of these elements of nature have I'm sure been here for an eternity whereas we on the other hand have not'. They both fell silent now left to their own thoughts and aspirations as the train thundered on relentlessly, taking Richard to Cornwall and David to his crabs in Cromer.

'Tickets please' said a voice that abruptly brought them both back to the mundane of everyday life. After clipping the relevant bits the inspector was gone leaving them in silence. Richard looked out the window and saw that the sloping plains and hills were now disappearing and replaced by low flat countryside and David's stop fast approached.

'Won't be long now before we get to Peterborough' said Richard.

'No' he replied now pushing his flask back into his rucksack and fastening the straps tightly' 'Well that's me ready. I have enjoyed meeting you so much and sharing such an illuminating time with you and will look out in the bee journals for news of your mapping endeavours, I wish you every success'.

'Thank you' said Richard 'And I hope you enjoy your stay in Cromer'. The train had now pulled into the station and as quickly as he had appeared he disappeared with his old rucksack on his back swinging to and fro as he made to his way to the exit and off the train, gone for ever. Richard leant out of the carriage window and thought that Peterborough station was a rather grey and depressing place with two platforms, the usual coffee shops and a passenger lounge where he spotted a few people waiting who he thought looked as depressed as the station. He spotted a figure in the overhead gantry between the platforms making a sprint to catch their train and a porter further down helping a young mother with her two children, a pushchair and a rather large sheep dog on board who seemed somewhat reluctant to jump the gap. As a last resort the owner gave a sharp tug on its lead and he watched its back legs fly out mid air as it embarked at last, accompanied now by loud screams from one of the children that slowly subsided as the carriage doors closed.

Richard was now on his own and had time to ponder his visit to St. Mawes. He thought about the bee mapping, Justin Blake and of course the trips. He would get to the Victory Inn, settle himself in, a nice evening meal and an early night he thought and then tomorrow morning breakfast and of course a trip. He must have dropped off to sleep then as a sudden jolt woke him up as they passed over a number of intersections and points as the train slowly lumbered into King's Cross station. Over the loudspeaker the calm efficient voice of a young woman announced that they had reached their final destination and reminded everyone to please make sure to take all their belongings with them, because if they were left behind they would have to be removed and may also in certain circumstances unfortunately have to be destroyed.

CHAPTER TWENTY-SIX

As the carriage doors opened Richard's senses were immediately invaded by the noise, heat and smell of London and he remembered all to well why he had been so pleased about their move to Durham. He heard the screams again of the child from earlier and looking up the platform now saw the young mother disembarking and quickly tying the dog lead on to the handle of the pushchair and frantically looking for someone behind the ticket barrier. Her face broke into a smile when she saw that that someone was there and now help was close at hand for her.

Richard slipped his ticket through the machine and now made his way across the very busy concourse joining the Friday throng who were all on their way somewhere for the weekend. He scanned the back wall of the station and near one of the exits saw the underground sign and weaved his through the bodies and down the escalator into the bowels of the earth. He needed the circle line that would take him to Paddington station and then his train straight down to Truro.

On the tube he encountered the sardine syndrome as he held on tight to one of the straps and looking at his fellow passengers detected a mixed bunch of people ranging from the professionals to artisans, all being transported in a metal tube through this subterranean world. Up above in that other world passed Baker Street, the home of that great detective Sherlock Holmes, and just a bit further on Madam Tussauds, home to the famous and infamous immortalised forever in their wax moulds for all to see. The train now started to slow down as the driver gradually applied the brakes and out of the total darkness they pulled into a neon lit platform where a tiled wall with large letters told him that he had arrived in Paddington.

A few moments later Richard scanned the departure board in the main station and was pleased to see that his train was on time and would depart at 1 o'clock. He yawned as the early start caught up with him and hoped he would be able to grab a few hours sleep on the rest of his journey. As it happened the train was partially empty and after finding a nice quiet corner he sat back and watched again as the grey city was replaced by the green countryside and rolling hills. He started to think about the bee mapping and was curious as to their possible success and wondered how much chance would play a part, the chance that to begin with you would be able to locate the right area to map them in the first place. Chance was a strange thing and in an almost bizarre way the master of a lot of things in life. Richard always considered the most momentous event in human history was the advent of civilization with the birth of writing, architecture, government and all the accompanying attributes, discovered by a very clever man called Vere Gordon Childe who called it the Neolithic Revolution, brought about by a climatic change when the earth warmed up some 10,000 years ago. Then on a far smaller scale he thought about Madeira wine, that was discovered by chance as a result of an unsold shipment being left on a vessel and exposed to excessive heat and movement. So many momentous things in life happened by chance and Richard found it quite disconcerting that our destiny on closer examination was not always quite what it seemed. Destiny, luck, chance, the words rolled around his head and eventually blackness as he slipped into oblivion.

'It's time to wake up sir' he heard a voice say as he came to and looked out the window and saw they were slowing down and the platform of a nearing station came into view. 'My you were out of it, I thought you were never going to come to. We're just coming into Truro and your journey ends here sir'. Richard couldn't believe he had slept all the way from London, he knew he felt tired but not that tired. He stretched and gathered his thoughts together and asked the conductor about getting to St. Mawes. 'No problem sir, plenty of taxis will be outside the front of the station, it's only a short journey, about 6 miles'.

Richard nodded his thanks and made ready to get off the train. The conductor was right about the taxis and after attracting the attention of one of the drivers who was engaged in deep conversation and almost an argument with one of the other drivers, Richard found himself in the back of a very neat and tidy car on his way out of the station enclosure and into the centre of town from where they picked up the main road to Falmouth. Richard leant forward and put his hands on the back of the front seat 'I need to get to St. Mawes'.

'Yes that's fine sir, we'll be turning off soon on the B3289 that leads straight into St. Mawes, where are you staying'.

'At the Victory Inn'.

'Oh you'll be fine there, Tom Mates and his wife run a very nice establishment and you'll be well looked after'. They had now left the town and once out on the open road the taxi driver accelerated quickly and Richard sat well back and fastened his seat belt.

'I did originally think about getting another train down to Falmouth and then a boat across to St. Mawes, to arrive venetian style'.

'What's that you said' the taxi driver replied half turning round.

'That I thought about getting the boat to St. Mawes'.

'No you'll be waiting forever, it's too early in the year and the service is very poor, once we get into early Summer there are plenty of boats but not yet'.

'Yes that's what I thought'.

'Are you here on holiday, if so you're lucky as the weather has been kind for this time of year'.

'No I'm working, I'm a scientist' said Richard.

'Oh, right you are' said the taxi driver as their conversation dried up and Richard took in the passing scenery as it flashed by. Once in St. Mawes Richard noticed that the driver still drove fast as he manoeuvred narrow streets, rotating the steering wheel quickly from left to right until they pulled up very sharply at a small whitewashed building with a tiny porched front door complete with hanging baskets and a sign over the front saying Victory Inn.

'Here you are safe and sound' said the driver. Richard thought only just as he handed over the fare and got out the taxi. The driver slammed the car in first gear and was gone as he watched him screech round a corner and then silence, no doubt back to complete the argument still unfinished. The little wooden front door creaked as Richard pushed it open and walked into a small reception room with huge overhead beams. At the counter he rang a little bell and waited until the owner of a very large grey beard appeared followed by a small plump woman.

'It must be Mr Fellowes' said the owner of the beard as he offered a large hand. 'This is my wife Bess, and yes we've heard all the jokes before'. Bess Mates thought Richard to himself and smiled.

'Yes I'm sure you have' he said.

'Come this way Mr Fellowes, I'll take you to your room' said Mrs Mates 'And your most welcome'. Richard dutifully followed Mrs Mates through another door in the hallway and up a small staircase down a little corridor until she reached the end of the passageway. 'Your in here' she said pushing open a small door and into a room that was quite delightful. 'This is always a favourite and I'm sure you will be most comfortable here, we call this the Trafalgar room'.

'Yes' said Richard as he dropped his holdall onto a large double bed covered with a pale green candlewick bedspread with matching coloured curtains and looked around him. 'I can see why it's so popular'. He moved to a small window that had a magnificent view across the bay.

'Beautiful isn't it' said Mrs Mates. Richard looked across a wide blue expanse of water to a far sandy beach with a backdrop of pines. Just off the shoreline were a flotilla of yachts their sails a blaze of colour bobbing about gently in the ebb and flow of the tide. 'I know you're here to work but if you have a spare bit of time I can highly recommend hiring a rowing boat, some of my guests and particularly those with youngsters love it as a day out. I could do you a picnic if you want, just let me know'. Richard needed no coaxing and told Mrs Mates that tomorrow morning he would do just that, with the picnic of course. After checking that he had everything he needed and if he wanted any more towels just to let her know, she disappeared back downstairs to make sure she told him that Mollie, her young kitchen maid, had made a start on the vegetables for tonight's dinner as quite often she didn't know her parsnip from her potato.

CHAPTER TWENTY-SEVEN

Downstairs in the Victory bar Richard was informed by the current occupant of the Jutland Room that their restaurant's bouillabaisse was second to none, thanks to the arrival of Pierre their new head chef from Brittany. Looking around him Richard thought that the bar had retained its character from many decades ago with a heavy patterned carpet, low beams and deep red banquettes. He ordered his favourite tipple, a large Jack Daniels and closed his eyes as he felt the fiery liquid in his mouth tempered by the cold of the ice cubes and thought that he was quite going to enjoy his new life style, albeit temporary, a few days in the North East and then a few days in the South West. Bess Mates had now joined her husband behind the bar and asked him if he wanted a table for dinner but Richard declined asking if he could please just have a bowl of their delectable fish soup at the bar.

Later as Richard mopped up the remnants of the fish soup with a large piece of bread the Jutland man raised his eyebrows and said 'Well was it up to scratch'.

'Yes, can't say I've tasted finer, even in France'.

'Where are you from'

'Oh originally London but now living in Durham. I'm down here for bee mapping over the next few days on the St. Just-in-Roseland Point'.

'Bee mapping eh' said the Jutland man as he managed to extract a piece of peanut that had got stuck in between one of the very large gaps in his teeth. 'You're here to try and save our jars of honey'.

'Yes something like that' replied Richard as he wiped his mouth with a napkin. 'Are you here on holiday.

'Yes and no really, there's a family party and with so many of us no room at the inn so to speak'. Richard nodded and finished off his Jack Daniels.

'Well nice meeting you, early start tomorrow and all that so might see you again'.

'Yes maybe, well goodnight to you and oh happy bee hunting'. Richard gave a small smile and made his way back to his room and after undressing took one last look out of the window at the bay that was now pitch black except for a few pinpricks of light from a full moon overhead. He drew the curtains and got into bed not forgetting to set his alarm for 7 a.m. and an early breakfast with the prospect of a morning's rowing in front of him.

The breakfast proved as successful as his dinner the previous evening and Mrs Mates duly delivered the picnic as promised to his table as he finished his last cup of coffee. 'You'll find Ro Moore just along the front and he'll sort you out with a boat'. Richard smiled to himself and wondered if this name thing was a peculiarity of the area.

'Yes thanks, just along the front you say'. Bess Mates nodded and Richard picked up the small basket complete with linen cloth and disappeared upstairs to collect his belongings, plus of course finally the slim blue box that now contained a syringe full of bee venom.

He found Ro Moore in a deckchair looking out across the bay towards the pine clad shoreline. 'Tis a beautiful sight' he said to Richard 'Those young kiddies always think there's treasure there and a few pirates' he added.

'Bess Mates said you could find me a rowing boat for the morning' said Richard.

'Ay no problem, have you rowed before'.

'Yes' said Richard, on the Serpentine actually in Hyde Park'.

'London eh' said Ro, that's a long way from here, could be the moon as far as I am concerned'. He stood up and beckoned Richard to follow him to a set of steps in the quay wall. 'She'll do you nicely' he said pointing to a medium sized green boat. 'Don't worry about paying now, settle up with me when you get back'.

Richard thanked him and carefully navigated the steep steps down to the water front and placed his rucksack and lunch basket in the back of the boat. The sun had now come out and he removed his waterproof and rolled up his sleeves. 'When you get mid stream be careful as sometimes we get some strong currents, just keep the oars steady and you'll be fine'. Richard gave a small salute and pushed away from the quayside and carefully manoeuvred the boat further out. As he pulled at the oars he tried to remember when he had actually last rowed and decided that it must have been in his early twenties when he was at college in London, the pre Susan days. It all came back to him now as he recalled Stephanie, a young fine arts student with long blond hair and very straight teeth whom he had spent a brief summer flirtation. The small harbour began to shrink as Richard pulled hard on the oars and his tiny bedroom window at the Victory Inn shrank to a small dot. Nearby a little yacht with bright red sails was tacking a path across the bay and the owner of the vessel clad in a nautical blue jumper gave him a waive to which Richard returned a small salute. He counted about seven other vessels some of whom were making their way over to the point and the others out into Falmouth Bay and the open sea beyond.

Some fifteen minutes later Richard had reached half way across the channel and he heard the sudden scream of a flock of seagulls that were now circling the back of the yacht with red sails. Richard saw the owner of the vessel toss over the side what seemed to be the remnants of some earlier fishing, they swooped and dived for the tasty morsels fighting amongst themselves for the larger prize.

Watching the gulls feed reminded Richard of his own lunch and he pulled the oars onto the boat and reached for the little basket carefully removing the linen cloth to find a huge Cornish pasty nestling underneath. He took a bite and savoured its delectable filling, so different from the commercial rubbish he thought as he chewed and turned his face to the now very warm sun feeling totally relaxed and at one with the world. As Richard popped the last piece of the pasty into his mouth and brushed the crumbs off his front, he saw that Mrs Mates had included a healthy dessert, a large red apple that he decided to keep for later. Of in the distance he heard the steady boom of a canon that told him it was midday and the time had come, now come for his trip. He reached for his rucksack and the slim blue box containing the syringe with its potent liquid and taking it into his hand plunged the needle through deep soft flesh into a large blue vein below. He wondered this time if his transportation would be quicker but did not notice any perceptible difference until he felt that the warm sun had disappeared and a decided chill now encompassed him.

The large bay was no more and instead he looked across a still muddy coloured lake. Over the far side he instantly recognised the mill house with its large wheel still turning, he was on Malham Tarn. The sky was dark grey and the trees around the lake were in the early throes of Autumn, their leaves an array of vibrant reds and browns. On his last visit it was mid Summer but some three months had now elapsed within the space of just over a week or so. The sound of voices carried over the water from a boat some fifty feet away, its occupants were Conan and Adolphus, always present, always there. Adolphus was pointing at the water and Conan grabbed the oars and pulled hard nearer towards him. Richard leaned forward and peered into the water and spotted a fishing net that had caught fast in some weeds and watched as Conan leant over the side of the boat and stretched as far as he possibly could but to no avail.

'Use this pole to try and free the net' said Adolphus moving closer behind Conan peering over his shoulder. 'You should be able to reach it'. Conan manoeuvred the pole placing it through the net and pulled hard but nothing could dislodge it from its snare. 'Let me try, I have longer arms than you' said Adolphus now taking the pole and pushing it through the dark murky waters below. Conan rose from his crouched position at the front of the boat and tried to move nearer the side to give Adolphus more room but in so doing he seemed to lose his balance and all at once fell overboard and Richard watched helplessly as the cold dark water quickly encircled his body and he disappeared from sight. Adolphus abandoned the pole and now clutched at the side of the boat as he leant over shouting Conan's name over and over again with a terrified expression on his face. Richard without further thought leapt into the water and after taking a deep breath submerged beneath the surface and dived below but no light penetrated these waters, not even from the grey skies overhead and he could see nothing. After a few minutes his lungs felt as if they were going to burst and with a kick rose to the surface coughing and fighting for air. Looking up he saw Adolphus still frantically scanning the water and Richard with a few strokes was by the side of their boat and watched as Adolphus stretched out his arms to try and pull him onboard. He reached up but instead of feeling the bare skin of Adolphus' arms he now felt what was the heavy texture of wool instead and, opening his eyes, saw the heavy blue knitted nautical jumper that was inhabited by none other than the owner of the little yacht with bright red sails.

CHAPTER TWENTY-EIGHT

'Hold on fast, I've got you' said a strong confident voice 'Just grip tight and we'll soon have you out of there'. Richard squinted his eyes at the sudden bright sunlight and saw around him the bay once more and nearby his empty rowing boat bobbing around in the water. 'You got caught in a strong current and panicked, you're not the first and certainly won't be the last'.

'No' Richard croaked 'Thank you for coming to my rescue, it all happened so quick'.

'Yes it's like that nature, always catches us unawares'.

'My boat' said Richard 'We need to catch her'.

'No worries, I'll throw a rope and tow you both back safely to terra firma'. Richard smiled weakly and sat down starting to feel cold now and quite sick as well, it must have been that pond water or was it he thought to himself, he couldn't be sure of anything any more. He heard the sound of a motor and turned to see a large cloud of smoke rise from the back of the yacht. 'Thought she was going to let me down there, don't use it that often you see, with the tacking. We need to get you back asap, I'll get a rug for you'. The blue jumper disappeared through a hatch below and

Richard held tightly to the side of the vessel as she quickly ploughed her way through the waves and back towards dry land.

Ro Moore was waiting at the top of the quay stairs as were a lot of other onlookers who had witnessed the incident earlier. Richard after thanking his rescuer profusely and telling him that he must come to the Victory Inn bar for a drink one evening, collected his belongings as he walked back through the boat and onto the stairs. At the top of the quay Ro told him not to worry about the money and to get back to the Inn straight away where Bess would look after him. One of the witnesses to the incident said that one minute he was in the boat and the next in the water, but he hadn't seen what Richard had and that was a man drowning and who probably now was at the bottom of the lake and despite every effort on his part could not save him from a watery grave. Richard felt sad, although he had never spoken to Conan he truly believed that he was a good man and did not deserve the cruel fate that had been dealt him, and what about Adolphus who must have been devastated. He felt someone grab his arm and looked up at Ro's weather beaten face 'You've had a bad shock there, come on lad I'll see you're alright'.

Back at the Victory Inn Richard had now stopped shivering as he sipped a mug of hot sweet tea. Bess Mates looked at him anxiously but he assured her that the only thing hurt was his pride and maybe he wasn't such a good sailor as he thought. Ro took the opportunity to have a quick tot and was gone whilst Jim Mates shepherded a few onlookers out of the bar who had gathered around and told them that the show was over.

After Richard had retired to his room, for the rest of the day so he said, Bess and Jim Mates were busy in the kitchen as they made a start on the seafood for the evening's menu. Over the crab claws Bess casually said 'You know there's something I don't quite understand'.

'What's that love' said Jim as he extracted a particularly reluctant piece of crab.

'Well you know how Mr Fellowes said he got caught in the strong current'.

'Yes' said Jim. There was a slight pause until Bess said.

'But I don't see as how that can be because by all accounts he was nowhere near mid stream when it happened'.

'Well the chap who rescued him thought that was what happened'.

'That's as maybe but I'm not sure, it all seems a bit strange to me, mysterious'.

'Mysterious in what way'.

'Well if I knew that it wouldn't be mysterious would it' Bess said.

'I think it's best if you don't mention this to anybody else, just between you and me, ok'. Bess silently nodded her head as she applied the crackers to another claw and placed it into a large bowl ready for Jim's attention.

Upstairs in the safety and security of his room Richard thought about the day's events and kept going over things in his mind torturing himself that he hadn't been able to save Conan. But, thought Richard, could he have saved him anyway remembering that whenever there was any contact with anything, just a touch or the merest brush he came back. He heard a knock on the door and opened it to Bess with a large tray of tea and some of her homemade scones. She asked if he was alright and secured an order from him for the chef's special tonight, devilled crab served with wedges of lemon and a watercress salad that Richard said sounded delightful and he couldn't wait.

Later down in the bar he encountered the Jutland man who regaled him with full details of the family party earlier in the day, it was his sister's 60th birthday and what a surprise it had all been for her as she had had no idea of the plans. After a sip of his pint he looked at Richard and said 'And I understand that you've had an exciting day as well, a mid channel rescue no less'. Richard felt awkward about these public performances he seemed to be putting on, first the debacle in the restaurant, then the incident at Fountains Abbey and now this, what more was there to come he wondered.

'Oh it was something and nothing, I just wasn't such a good sailor as I thought, that's all'. The Jutland man took another pull at his pint and looked thoughtfully at him.

'Bit of confusion over the story as to what actually happened, some say it was mid channel and others maybe not'.

'Is that so' said Richard 'Well it doesn't really matter, does it, I survived and am here to prove it'. Changing the subject quickly he said 'Are you partaking of the devilled crab, the special tonight'.

'Yes I am, want to join me'.

'No you're alright, I'm dining in my room, a la tray actually and then an early night. Been nice meeting you though, take care'. Richard took his leave of the Jutland man and once more in his room was left to his thoughts and more importantly planning the next trip which would be after his meeting tomorrow with Justin Blake. A free afternoon beckoned and in the confines of his room he would do a trip and after that he would have to wait and see.

Richard looked up at the clock in the Victory Inn bar and at exactly midday the little oak wooden door opened and admitted Justin Blake. At first sight he struck him as the perennial student in a duffel coat and dishevelled shoulder length sandy coloured hair. By his side was a woman of older years smartly dressed and with a certain air, what did they call it, je ne sais quoi. He looked in Richard's direction and his face broke into a smile as he came over and held out his hand. 'It's Richard isn't it'.

'Yes it is, but how did you know'.

'Well unless BBKA have started emploing octogenarians'. Richard laughed and looking around at the other occupants in the bar saw what he meant. 'This is my mother, Jane and she has come to my rescue today as my old car seems to have finally given up the ghost. Richard saw in front of him a tall attractive woman, about mid fifties he guessed who had taken good care of herself.

'I kept telling him to get another one but he never listens to me and says that I just nag him'. Justin gave a small laugh.

'She's right of course, unfortunately obstinacy is one of my vices that apparently I have inherited from my father'.

'Oh he's even worse than you Justin, no although you're difficult you are manageable which he certainly is not'.

'So thanks to her usual generosity and her old Morgan we're here. Mind you she drives like a maniac, but'. Justin left the conversation mid sentence as Jane had just spotted an old school friend who had come into the inn and informed them that she would leave them to talk shop but that she would love a dry white wine.

'Quite a character, your mother' said Richard.

'Yes, isn't she and I love her to bits. Just let me get some drinks and we'll make a start'. Some moments later with their drinks in front of them and a large dry white wine safely deposited to his mother in the corner, Justin opened up his laptop and looked at Richard. 'Well here we are. I don't know how much you know about bee mapping or bee lining but I have located via our good friend Google an aerial view of the Val Estuary, and in particular some riverside gardens with semi-tropical plants, a possible habitat for our bees. It is known as the St Just creek in a setting with a 13th century church called appropriately St Just the Martyr that was once described by Sir John Betjeman, our famous Poet Laureate, as the most beautiful on earth. It has a lot of historical connections including the legend that this was where Joseph of Arimathea brought Jesus ashore. Anyway I am hoping that this site will prove fruitful, but I am reminded here of the immortal words of Winnie the Pooh who said you never can tell with bees'. Richard smiled to himself quite liking his new acquaintance who although totally dedicated was blessed with a sense of humour.

'So what do I have to do'.

Justin reached into his bag and pulled out a map 'This Richard is a print out of the area you need to search, I've marked the exact location here'. Richard leant forward and familiarised himself with the spot. 'You will set up three bait stations by placing an aluminium pan filled with rocks on a cardboard box, around the rocks you need to pour some sugar water or honey. Repeat this process every fifty yards or so in a straight line. Now comes the more difficult part as you will need to catch honey bees and then release them at each of the bait stations where they will fill up on the sugar water or honey and then fly in a straight line back to the colony. Hopefully they will also bring their bee friends back for more. Are you o.k. so far'. Richard nodded and waited for Justin to continue. 'You will need to observe the bees and take a note of the direction they fly in from the bait station, this is known as the bee line. Now you will need to take your map and draw a straight line from each of the bait station locations along each bee line from the bait stations, this will allow you to triangulate the approximate location of the colony, the colony is likely to be where the lines intersect'. He sat back and looked at Richard. 'Are you happy with that'.

'Yes, it seems quite basic really but successful I take it'.

'Oh yes, tried and tested. The only piece of advice I can offer really is be patient, after you have set up the bait stations it can be a bit of a wait sometimes, take a sandwich, take a book'. Richard thought to himself that he would take a trip, it really looked quite a secluded area and another opportunity. 'Now the only other thing of course is transport, I was going to pick you up but as I am now without wheels so to speak suggest you take a taxi, it's not too far'.

'Yes no problem, when will we meet up again'.

'I'm working another area but will come over and meet up with you tomorrow at the creek, say 1 o'clock'. Richard agreed and they both wished each other happy hunting or mapping as the case may be. Justin looked over at his mother who was still chatting to her friend and told her that it was time to make a move. 'She'll be there all night, you see Jane is a great bridge player and her friend is too, they're playing at a tournament in Bristol next week so get them together and they will be discussing tactics all night. Jane kissed her friend on the cheek and arrived back at the table and held her hand out to Richard.

'So nice to meet you, I'll get Justin to bring you over for a meal some time and we can have a proper chat, until then'. Just as quickly as they had arrived they were gone and Richard was left quite alone apart from one or two stragglers left nursing the remainder of their pints and then home to a Sunday roast. Jim and Bess did not provide food at lunchtime as Pierre, their temperamental chef constantly reminded them, that he was not God and it was only possible that he could ever achieve one creation in any given day.

CHAPTER TWENTY-NINE

Richard found the silence deafening as he lay on his bed upstairs, he had heard the last of the lunchtime drinkers depart, the bolt shot across the little wooden oak front door and then nothing.

He looked down at the empty syringe in his hand and then out across the bay and in an abstract way tried to see if he could spot the little yacht with its bright red sails but there was no time, because in the blink of an eye he had gone back, back to that other time. The small window he had been looking out of had now disappeared and replaced by a large mullioned one, the view of the calm blue sea was no more and instead he saw what was the now familiar dark green of the cloister lawn. Turning round he immediately recognised the chapter house with its grey three tiered stone platform and large chair set in a huge niche at the far end. His thoughts went back to, when was it, only a matter of weeks but it felt like months ago he had been here before at that meeting with Linus Deyer and the others, all of whom had now been banished apart from Prior Heribert. The sound of voices could now be heard that got louder and louder, Richard peered through the window to see a group of brothers fast making their way towards the door and he moved back to one side waiting to see what happened next.

As they entered the chapter house he observed their faces noting that he only recognised two of them, Prior Heribert and Adolphus, the latter who for the first time was on his own proving undeniably in Richard's mind that Conan was dead and his body lying somewhere deep under the water on the bed of Malham Tarn. He detected a certain lethargy about Adolphus, gone now was the carefree expression and replaced by a gaunt one, his back once straight and erect was now slightly stooped.

'Brethren I fear we face a cold harsh winter, this October has brought us holly bushes with a bountiful supply of berries and a harsh wind too'. Richard took a quick breath and calculated that within the space of just twenty-four hours another month must have passed already. The one who delivered the foreboding weather now took his pride of place in the large chair which confirmed this was Henry Cuylter, the new Abbot. He was much younger than Linus Deyer, maybe somewhere in his mid 40's with a willowy physique and a fine mane of dark hair.

'Tis true Abbot, the trees in the valley are heavily clothed with miseltoe and much to the rooks' delight as well'. Richard looked at the brother who spoke but did not recognise him. The Abbot now directed his gaze at Adolphus and after a few moments deliberation cleared his throat and said.

'Brother we feel your sorrow and pray for the departed soul of Brother Conan, taken from us so suddenly and in such a cruel manner, untimely as well'. He looked behind the huddle in front of him until his eyes rested on a figure lurking at the back of the group and Richard following his eyes picked out a diminutive figure with his eyes cast to the ground. 'Brother Milo, I am appointing you as helper to Brother Mathias, he will teach you well in the art of bees'. The small figure now lifted his eyes and said in a small quiet voice.

'Yes of course Abbot'. The group turned and looked at Brother Milo and then back at the Abbot murmuring under their breath and Richard was sure that he heard the word bastard. He felt shocked and deduced that this poor creature was the result of some out of wedlock liaison and he in turn muttered hypocrites under his breath.

'Now brethren' began the Abbot, 'Some months have now lapsed since the departure of some of our previous brothers who sadly broke God's law in their administrations and may we pray for their souls.'Tis a fact though that they disgraced and plunged us into debt but slowly we make amends with our coffers starting to fill again'. His keen eyes scanned the group in front of him again and this time rested on a tall lean figure. 'Sacrist Leybourne has greatly assisted me brothers in the pursuit of an artefact that will greatly benefit us' he paused slightly before adding 'a holy relic'. The brothers gasped and looked at each other in turn waiting for the Abbot to continue. 'As we all know Thomas Beckett was struck down in Canterbury Abbey fifteen years ago and afterwards his body was kept safe in one of the chapels. The name of the monk who tended his body has never been revealed safe to say that he cut a piece of material from his robe, a bloodied piece of cloth. That piece of cloth is now in our possession and will become a shrine that pilgrims will revere and bring to it their oblations'. Richard pondered on the reaction of the King to this piece of news because of his hand in the death of Thomas Beckett and thought that it would not sit well with him. 'The shrine will be in the chapel of St. James the Great in the care of Sacrist Leybourne, and his sub-sacrist will sit guard at night to ward off any would be robbers whom I fear will go to great lengths to steal our relic.' The brothers all nodded their heads in agreement and waited for the Abbot to continue. 'Fountains Abbey will receive many pilgrims as news spreads over the land and to shores afar'. He paused slightly to look out of the window before continuing. 'I have knowledge that the piece of cloth has healing powers, some who have touched it have been cured of their ills, a miracle no less'. Brother Adolphus now moved to the front and cleared his throat.

'Abbot 'tis well known that honey has healing properties that I have used to treat many of our brothers with their ailments. May we Abbot place jars of honey before the shrine that would then become infused with miraculous healing powers'. The Abbot gazed at Adolphus and gently nodded his head.

'Yes brother, the pilgrims will take away with them a divine potion and we the better off with their offerings'. The conversation stopped as they heard the sound of a loud thud on the chapter house window and they turned to see a large black raven furiously beating its wings against the glass. In a second the black wings had become white and Richard saw a seagull with the sun penetrating its wings and the pink tracery of its veins through a strong shaft of sunlight, he had come back. He slipped off the bed and went to the window to briefly glimpse the huge open orange beak of the bird before it took flight and watched as it flew off into the afternoon sun to its lair or in search of food. He went over the conversation he had heard in the chapter house and as always fervently hoped he would be party to the next stage of events, something he could never be sure of.

The rest of the day passed uneventfully apart from a telephone call from Susan who told him that things had now sorted themselves out and she would see him at home early next week. He would be going home on the Wednesday morning which he knew would buy him a bit more time, two more days to be precise. He went over in his mind the conversation with Justin and a quick reference to the bee mapping notes and knew nothing further till the alarm on his mobile phone went off at 8 a.m. the next morning.

He found Bess Mates up to her armpits in fried eggs and bacon in the kitchen and reassured her that he would not go hungry and would probably pick up some breakfast en route to St Justin-Roseland to fortify himself for the day ahead. His taxi arrived promptly at the front door of the Victory Inn at 9 o'clock and, despite his instructions to the driver, was reliably informed that he knew where he was going and no need to worry. The journey passed in a flash of dark green hedgerows and yellow fields till the car pulled up sharply at St Just Creek and was told that they had reached their destination and he owed ten pounds.

It took Richard a few minutes to assemble himself with a large rucksack and holdall that contained all the pans and rocks, plus of course the sugared water to entice the black honeybees. After a quick waive to the driver Richard looked around him and saw before him a tree lined creek with a church set in an ampitheatre like graveyard filled with an array of colourful sub tropical plants and shrubs. He heard the last of the taxi's engine as it navigated the very tight bend at the top of the road and then there was silence and with it came a certain peace and tranquillity. The sun had now started to shine quite brightly and the earlier clouds disappeared, it looked like it was going to be a good day, a good day for his bee mapping. Richard took in his surroundings and began to work out the location for the three bait stations remembering Justin's instructions that one should be cited every 50 to 100 yards. He looked around him noting the bright shades of various plants and believed that the mixture of colour and sugar water would surely prove an irresistible combination to the bees. He walked for a few minutes towards the waters edge in the creek and crouched down to open up his rucksack. He removed one of the pans and started to fill it with rocks finally pouring a concoction of sugar and water around them. He retraced his steps and after approximately 50 metres repeated the same process again and scanning the air around him wondered how long it would take for the bees to arrive. As it happened he didn't have to wait too long because as he placed the last pan down among some shrubs he heard a loud buzzing noise and looked up to see a small group of bees busy nestling among some massive flower heads in search of nectar. 'Oh my beauties do I have a banquet ready for you'. He had some plastic boxes ready that he now used to catch each of the bees and released them separately at the three bait stations, there was nothing he could do now but wait and see what happened.

He heard the sound of approaching voices and saw two young lads bantering with each other as they made their way towards him playfully pushing each other until they drew level with Richard. After eyeing him up and down the elder of the two stepped forward and said 'Hello mister, what are you doing'.

'I'm searching for bees, a colony to be precise and you might just be able to help me'.

'How's that then'.

'Follow me and I'll show you'. Richard beckoned to the two lads who looked at each other and then fell in close behind him until they reached the furthest bait station where the bee still slurped happily at the sweet liquid in the bottom of the pan. 'There are two other containers like this and I need you to watch where the bees fly off to, we can each watch one of the bait stations and with any luck we'll see where they go, look very carefully'. The boys despite their earlier vague curiosity were now quite enthused by the whole thing and stood near their post with eyes firmly locked and all was silent. 'Look mine's flown away' shouted the younger boy.

'Which direction' said Richard.

'Over towards the church'.

Within the same space of time the other two bees had followed and Richard beckoned them over to his rucksack for stage two of the procedure. 'Do you know a lot about bees mister'. Richard glanced up and smiled them.

'I should do, I'm what's known as a bee specialist, my speciality is viruses, you see bees get ill just like us'.

'Are these bees ill'.

'No, this is different. You see the bee population is declining, getting smaller' he added. 'We're trying to catch wild black honeybees to increase the number of bees we have, does that make sense'.

'Yes, it does. So what are you doing now'. Richard spread out on the grass a map and with his pencil and ruler drew straight lines from each of the bait stations that confirmed their visual location some few hundred yards away by the church. 'Together we have located a colony, by the way what are your names'.

'I'm Ben' said the elder of the two 'And this is Jason. Have we really helped you'.

'Yes you have and future generations will thank the likes of you'. The boys smiled at each other and looked very proud.

'We'll have to go now, our mums will be wondering where we are' said Ben.

'Yes boys, take care and remember the next time you eat honey'.

'That we helped to make it' said Jason who had now started to come out of his shell.

'Yes something like that' said Richard. The boys now made their way back down the path and continued with their banter of pushing and shoving until they disappeared from view. Richard felt very pleased with himself, not forgetting his two young helpers of course and laid back on the grass. He closed his eyes and felt the warm sunlight on his face, time was now his own and a trip beckoned. Sitting up he reached into a side pocket of his rucksack and pulled out the slim blue box and opened it wide carefully removing one of the syringes. He looked up in the sky as he plunged it into his arm until he no longer saw the blue heavens above him but the orange watery coloured sky of a late winter's afternoon.

CHAPTER THIRTY

He felt the sensation of a deep penetrating cold and sat up to see the ground was covered in a light layer of snow that had fallen recently. He regretted that he had no coat but remembered he had peeled it off and thrown it to one side in that warm afternoon sun, back in that other time. He shivered and rubbed his hands together and was aware of the sound of low murmuring voices and saw over by the porch of the abbey a large crowd of people who stood shuffling their feet in the snow in an attempt to keep warm.

Richard stood up and brushed the snow of his back and walked towards them. Looking down at the ground he noticed that as he walked there were no footprints left behind him, not a trace that he had ever been there, no sign of his mortal presence. Again in his mind he pondered the huge time differences that now seemed to be happening every time he came back, months seem to have passed by in just a day or so. Before it had been October and now, well he guessed it was probably late November or early December, were the big leaps in time connected with the dosage, was he now injecting himself with more venom than that by a sting. He gave a small inward cringe as the Professor's words echoed in his ears when he told him that he was poisoning himself, just how much of this stuff had he taken.

He wondered why they were all waiting at the abbey door and soon learnt the answer as he heard a small group of them discuss the distances they had travelled to visit the holy shrine and see the relic. Yes of course, the bloodied piece of cloth from the robe of Thomas Beckett, these were the pilgrims that the Abbot had spoken about.

'I left Rutland some weeks ago, I have suffered terrible with my leg but hope some of the divine miraculous healing powers will restore some good'. Another said.

'I left the South, ay by the channel even further away, from Netley Abbey. I bring many petitions from the faithful as well as a good pouch of money'. What sweet words they would be to the Abbot thought Richard, money for the coffers, his plan had worked well. But why were they waiting outside, was the queue so long they had to wait their turn.

Richard walked through them as a ghost and silently pushed the door open to reveal that the inside of the abbey was empty, no queues, no chatter but only the sound of a chant of Veni, Veni Emmanuel that Richard knew even with his scant knowledge of latin meant 'O Come, O Come Emmanuel', it was Christmas or in their time Michelmas. The sweet smell of mistletoe and holly filled his nostrils and the knowledge that it was neither late November or early December come to that. His silent steps took him through the nave where a few monks knelt in prayer until he passed the north transept to his left and the choir to his right as the faithful chanted their Christmas song over and over again, a slow mesmerizing chant. Richard had poured endlessly over plans of the abbey interior and knew that his destination lay some 100 yards to the left and also whatever it was that kept the pilgrims freezing outside. The interior of the abbey was quite dark and lit only by a sea of dim candles and what little light there was from outside filtered through the stained glass windows high above. At the end of the nave, just beyond the High Altar, he saw a group of figures cordoning off the Chapel of the Nine Altars leading to the Chapel of St. James the Great and the shrine. As he approached he saw they were clad in chain mail armed with swords and shields, obviously a guard but protecting what Richard wondered and quickly deduced that this was no ordinary guard and certainly not one mounted by the Abbot, but what the hell was it.

Unlike others whose path would have been easily barred, he slipped past them and saw around the corner the chapel of St. James brightly lit by a huge bank of candles that rose from the floor around the stone altar reaching to the wall at the back. Richard shielded his eyes as he found the light quite blinding after the relative dimness of the abbey and saw as his eyes adjusted a figure kneeling at the foot of the altar who he recognised immediately as King Henry, no wonder the protective guard. Richard now stood right beside him and no longer saw a proud looking King but a half bent pathetic man beating his chest and muttering to himself. He leant nearer and caught the words 'Will no one rid me of this turbulent priest' repeating the words over and over again. The priest he referred to was St. Thomas Beckett, now the bane of his life and the shrine that sought his unequivocal repentance. His murmurings stopped as his eyes lifted up to a small wooden box set high up in the altar at arms length and out of reach. Richard moved nearer and stood on tiptoe as his eyes gazed on the contents, a small piece of cloth with a dark brown stain, the relic from the bloodied robe of St. Thomas on which it seemed so much depended. Richard wondered if this truly was from the robe of Thomas Beckett and felt a sudden religious pang as his knees bent beneath him and he bent his head to pray. Before he closed his eyes he spotted at the foot of the altar numerous pots that he knew without looking contained the honey that Adolphus asked could be placed there, the special honey with miraculous healing powers. He picked up one of the stone jars and peered over the rim to look inside as he heard a voice say.

'Richard, what are you doing, it looked as if you were praying'. Richard swung round to see Justin standing behind him with a bemused expression on his face.

'I was just looking at the pots of honey' and immediately the words had left his lips he realised how strange it must have sounded.

'What pots Richard' said Justin now starting to sound quite concerned. 'You were looking at one of the pans with sugar water'. Richard's return this time had just seemed so instantaneous and he struggled to get himself together.

'Yes, well it is a kind of honey isn't it, but just in a more basic form'. He stood up and pointed over towards the church, 'That's where I've located a colony, I was very lucky actually as a couple of young lads helped me watch the bee lines and I've marked the map'. He spread the map out on the ground and pointed to the triangulation area, 'It all ties in, the visual and the geometrics'. Justin peered at the map and over towards the church.

'You've done well Richard, and a first go as well, you must be a natural at this'. Richard smiled feeling very pleased with himself.

'Yes I must be'. Justin stared at Richard as he ran his hand through his hair.

'Are you alright though, I mean that business about the pots of honey just now, big strange'.

'I get so enthused sometimes with my work, say a few silly things but it doesn't mean anything'. Justin continued to stare at him and then gently nodded his head.

'Yes, I suppose I'm the same sometimes, this enthusiasm just takes over. You know Richard you've done a cracking job here so if you want to call it a day on this visit and get back home that's fine, and we'll see you again next week'.

'Yes that suits me. By the way how did you get on with your mapping, any luck'.

'No, not today, I'll try another site tomorrow. I'll take all the information now though that you have and pass it on so that the work can start straight away on collecting the bees from that colony, well done again'.

The following morning, after on this occasion one of Bess Mates huge cooked breakfast and a confirmation that he would be back again next Sunday, Richard made his way back home to No. 27 Hereford Row arriving at his front door late afternoon. Susan's car was parked in the driveway and he heard her singing along to the radio as he dumped his bags on the hall floor. 'You sound happy love' said Richard as he found her up to her arms in dirty washing. She reached out and gave him a hug and told him she was so pleased to be back home again and that he looked tired but wanted to know all the news about his bees. Over a cup of tea he relayed to her from beginning to end his trip to St. Mawes leaving out of course his near death experience in the bay, he would leave that part of the story until he spoke to the Professor.

'Are you working tomorrow Richard' she asked 'I thought he might go shopping together'. He thought to himself that shopping was the last thing on his mind as he said.

'I need to go into the office to sort out some notes from this trip, let's go at the weekend'. She gave a small shrug and continued to feed the washing machine reminding him to let her have his laundry after he had unpacked. Upstairs he carefully secreted the slim blue box at the back of his underwear drawer and planned that he would go into the office for another supply of venom and then to the library to see the Professor. He felt a sudden sharp pain in his arm and rolled up his sleeve to see that the area he had been injecting himself looked very sore and swollen, it looked infected. He hadn't heard the bedroom door open but he now heard a gasp as he saw Susan in the reflection of a mirror.

'My God Richard, what's happened to your arm'. She swiftly moved over to him and inspected it.

'Oh a bee sting, have you got any onions'.

'That looks like it needs more than an onion, it needs the casualty department. Come on let's go to the hospital'. Richard pulled his arm away but Susan was adamant that somebody should look at it and he reluctantly gave in. Two hours later in the local a and e department a young doctor examined him and said that he had never seen anything like it before and would clean it up and do some blood tests just to be on the safe side. Richard's heart was pounding as he wondered exactly what the tests would show, remembering the Professor's comments about this toxic cocktail but now there was nothing further he could do and he would just have to wait for events to unfold. Back home he told Susan that he would sleep in the spare room that night as his arm was very painful and he may be restless and didn't want to disturb her any more than he had to.

His visit to the office in the morning was a quick one, luckily Piers was out for the day so he did not have to face a debriefing session about the mapping for which he was grateful. His main priority was to obtain more venom, a task which proved a quick exercise as he quickly filled four phials with the colourless liquid and then left the building immediately. His steps now headed towards the library, he had not wanted a debriefing session with Piers but he desperately wanted one now with the Professor and it could not wait.

An hour later he breathed a sigh of relief as he turned the corner into the history section of the library and saw the Professor at his desk and it was as if with some sixth sense he looked up straight at him and said 'I've been waiting for you, I knew you would come'.

'I've just back from St. Mawes, and'.

'You want to tell me what happened'.

'Yes, can we talk'. The Professor pulled a chair over to his desk and motioned him to sit down.

'I take it that you are still tripping'. Richard lowered his eyes and felt quite guilty but helpless somehow.

'Yes and I had a lucky escape'. He then told the Professor at great length and in great detail not forgetting anything about his trips and finally ended with his visit to the hospital and how worried he was about what the blood tests might show.

'I think Richard you must know that something is going to show up but what they will make of it I don't know, that you are being poisoned but how. He fell silent for a few moments and then continued. 'Perhaps you should just make a clean breast of it, I don't know what else you can do'. Richard now fell silent as well before saying.

'But that means I won't be able to do any more trips, you see I just have to, I can't stop'.

'What even if that means you will die'. Neither of them now said anything at all and Richard sensed their conversation was over, that their relationship somehow was at a end.

'Thank you Professor for listening to me, for being my friend however brief it has been, I must go now'. He held out his hand and the Professor gripped it firmly saying.

'Good luck my boy, good luck'. He watched as Richard walked away and knew he would never see him again. What he hadn't told him though was that when the black raven had thrown itself against the chapter house window it was a portent of death, the horrible inescapable fact that he was going to die and very soon.

CHAPTER THIRTY-ONE

Back at home in the kitchen Richard found Robyn and Susan talking excitedly about her dancing trip to Dortmund.

'You know mum I competed against fifty other girls, and guess what I won'.

'You're a very clever girl though where you get this talent from I've no idea, certainly not from my side of the family, how about yours Richard'.

'I've really no idea but well done Robyn'.

'I'll need loads of stuff you know'.

'Yes we can sort things out' said Susan. 'Richard I see you've made a start on the materials for decorating, Robyn said her bedroom will soon be all gothic'.

'Best get my arm right first, then I'll get going with it'.

'Dad had a friend over the other evening' said Robyn her eyes looking at the floor 'It was really strange mum, I don't know what they were doing'. It was the conversation that Richard had dreaded and quickly said.

'Yes, Professor Durnley, from the local library. We've got a lot in common and we were just sharing our thoughts, that's all'. He wanted to play things down as quickly as possible and luckily it seemed had got away with it as Susan chatted on about Dortmund again and the moment had passed.

He managed to excuse himself early that night, on account of his arm, and retired to the spare room with his pyjamas and the slim blue box now replete with a new supply of venom. He read a magazine while he waited for Susan to come in and kiss him goodnight, then he could inject himself and take another trip. It seemed liked hours passed until eventually he saw the landing light turned off and the bedroom door quietly opened. 'Richard are you alright' she asked in a concerned way.

'Yes, just waiting to kiss my favourite girl goodnight'. She bent over the bed and kissed his forehead brushing his hair back at the same time.

'Sleep well my love'. He watched the door close and breathed a quiet sigh of relief as he pulled the slim blue box out from under his pillow and taking the syringe plunged it into his arm and waited. It seemed at first as if nothing was going to happen as he stared at the rays of light shining through the curtains from the lamp post outside in the street while he waited, waited for them to disappear. He turned over and pulled the duvet around his shoulders and sensed the soft texture of cotton had disappeared and been replaced instead by a rough crude like straw cover. The rays of the street light had now gone and he peered into what was total darkness. He raised himself up and listened to hear the sound of snoring beside him and realised he was not alone. Quietly he got out of bed and reached out to feel the covers of another bed and realised that he must have gone back to the monks dormitory and it was the middle of the night. He vaguely wondered if time had rushed on again and if so what season it might be. A bell started to ring in the background, slowly methodically and with it came the rustling noise of bodies around him rising from their slumber. Someone lit a candle and the faint glow illuminated the dim interior of his surroundings, a long rectangular room with a very low ceiling and rows of beds against either side of the walls. In the middle stood what looked like a long row of cupboards from which some of the monks now retrieved robes pulling the hoods tightly over their head. He shivered, it was freezing cold and unlike them only had his pyjamas to keep him warm.

Swiftly the hooded monks formed a line and waited till a muffled voice gave a command and the light of a lantern held aloft disappeared from the end of the dormitory. The monks slowly shuffled along and Richard followed them till he was at the top of a stairwell that he knew were the night stairs into the abbey and the near darkness slowly disappeared as the light from below crept up the walls around them. At the foot of the stairs the monks filed into the pews and Richard dutifully followed them. The bell that had rung so slowly and methodically now ceased and a soft chant of prayers began, the words to be repeated over and over again. Over towards the Chapel of St. James a long queue were waiting to pay their homage to the relic and, casting his eyes backwards, saw the line went right down the nave to the entrance into the abbey. It was now the pilgrims' turn to revere the bloodied piece of robe and he imagined that their homage would be far more peaceful than the King's had been, as Richard recalled the sight of him beating his chest with tears welling in his eyes.

The chanting prayers ceased and he turned back to see what would happen next but his eyes stopped midway, paralysed as he could not believe his eyes. He gulped shutting them and looked again, about four rows back he saw Adolphus with Conan sitting next to him. What the hell, Conan was dead, how, how could he be there. Richard started to panic and began screaming out loud 'But your dead, your dead, I saw you drown'.

He saw no more of the abbey, the pilgrims, Adolphus or Conan but only Susan bending over him looking absolutely terrified. 'Richard wake up, wake up, your having a nightmare, you said somebody had drowned. He fought to catch his breath aware that his heart was pounding in his chest and he was sweating profusely and his pyjamas that were now wet through clung to his body. Another thing he was aware of was that he was in agony and if he had been terrified before it was nothing as to the sight that now met his eyes. You could no longer call it an arm but an horrendous piece of flesh that hung from his shoulder from which pus ouzed with a terrible stench, he retched violently while Susan tried to restrain him. 'My God, my God, Richard lay still, don't move, an ambulance, I must get an ambulance'. The hand that now dialled 999 shook violently and she screamed at the operator that her husband was dying and they must come straight away. Between the bouts of vomiting he laid his head on the pillow still fighting for breath until a flashing blue light covered the ceiling above him going round and round until he gave in and lost consciousness.

He knew nothing of the mad dash to the hospital or of Susan just hanging on to his hand and crying. She knew that something had not been right with Richard for some time, was this her fault, could she have done something. The duty doctor in a small room at the side of the ward reliably informed her that there was nothing she could have done and asked her if she knew that her husband was a user.

'What do mean' she gasped.

'Mrs Fellowes your husband has been taking some type of drug. He came in yesterday as an out patient and we ran some blood tests, the results of which we were going to contact you urgently'. He paused as he read from a piece of paper in front of him and Susan sat numbly staring at him, it was like a nightmare. 'This drug he's been taking is toxic, we're not exactly sure what it is and will need to run some more tests before we can begin treating him'. Susan stared blankly at him.

'How long will it take, he's so ill'.

'We'll act on it immediately and until then all we can do is try to stabilise his condition'. Susan then uttered the words that she so dreaded.

'Is he, is he going to be alright'. The doctor reached over and patted her on the arm.

'Be sure we will do everything we can for him'.

'Can I see him'.

'Give us a few minutes Mrs Fellowes, we need to do a few things and then of course you can'. The doctor left her sitting in a daze and she thought that she ought to call her sister, she needed someone with her, she couldn't go through this on her own. But what was this about drugs, Richard had never touched them in his life, even in his young student days not so much as a joint. She pulled out her mobile phone and dialled her sister hoping that she was around and, also more importantly, could she come straight away.

Richard had now gained consciousness and lay on the bed vaguely aware of what was going on. At least the pain in his arm had now stopped after he had been given some very strong pain killers and he watched as the medics around performed various tasks. It seemed everything the Professor had told him was true but what now. A figure now appeared by Richard and he looked up at the face of the duty doctor who gave a small smile. 'Just try to relax Mr Fellowes, your wife will be in shortly'. He leant over Richard and gently shone a light into both of his eyes but it was no longer the face of the doctor that he saw in front of him but that of Adolphus. Richard tried to speak but no words came out of his mouth which had now started to dribble out of one corner. Adolphus leaned closer and whispered in his ear.

'Don't worry everything will be alright, we will take care of you, you are with us now'.